DOWN THE BIG RIVER

by STEPHEN W. MEADER

ILLUSTRATED BY EDWARD SHENTON

Purple House Press
Kentucky

Published by
Purple House Press
PO Box 787
Cynthiana, Kentucky 41031

Classic Books for Kids and Young Adults
purplehousepress.com

Written in 1924 by Stephen W. Meader, illustrations by Edward Shenton
Revised edition and new artwork © 2021 by Purple House Press

ISBN 9781948959728

Chapter I

A ROUGH-HAIRED little brown dog came trotting up the wilderness trail. He scouted in and out of the thickets and sniffed at the roots of the giant trees, then scampered on, out of sight. After him in a moment followed a white mare, her shoes clinking lightly on outcroppings in the trail as she climbed with sure, quick steps. A boy rode her, slouching in the saddle, his long, buckskin-clad legs hanging half a foot below the girth. He had on a bucksin top and coonskin cap, and in the crook of his arm lay a long-barrelled squirrel rifle. His face, for all its youth, was stern and tired.

At the top of the ascent the boy reined in his mare and halted, looking long and intently ahead at a little clearing in the trees on the next ridge. When he had finished he turned his mount and started back down the rough mountain trail.

"Get on with you, Pocono," he said. "Those lazy drivers will be stopping for the night if we don't tell them there's an inn ahead."

The sure-footed animal went scrambling down the slope, avoiding the stumps and roots that dotted the slashing, and came at length to the little stream that ran down the bottom of the ravine. She stopped with both forefeet in the water and flung her nose down to drink. The boy, starting to pull her up with an impatient tug on the rein, sat suddenly erect and swung half about in the saddle. The mare threw her head up and her haunches quivered. The sound they both had heard came from somewhere up the valley to the north. Even as they listened it was repeated—the faint, far-off hunting-call of a gray wolf.

The lad gathered the reins with a sharp gesture, and drove his moccasined heels into the flanks of his mare so that she started up the farther hillside with a jump. Out of the bushes alongside burst the little dog, growling low, and at a quiet command from his owner, followed close at the mare's heels.

It was already after sunset and only a faint glow of evening light shone through the bare branches of the great hardwood trees. The boy knew something of the wolf packs that ran in the Allegheny hills, and he was quite aware that they sometimes made things uncomfortable for winter travelers who camped in the open. Before the mare had covered half the distance to the top of the hill, however, her rider caught the sound of approaching wagon wheels and the occasional shout of teamsters, and he pulled his eager little mount to a stop by the trailside.

Over the crest came the wagons, canvas-topped and huge of wheel, swaying downward with a grind of brakes. There were two of these crude wilderness conveyances and each was drawn by six gaunt, big-boned horses. The patched harness and the mud-caked wheels bore witness to long hard weeks on the trail.

Beside the second wagon, on a roan horse, rode a man of middle age, dressed in stout gray homespun. His bearded face had an anxious look as he pulled up abreast of the boy on the white mare.

"Any sign of shelter, Tom?" he asked.

"A small inn, not more than a mile ahead, Uncle Ezra," the lad replied. "It's just as that freighter told us—not much to look at, but 'twill serve to keep those varmints out."

He turned, listening, as the distant wolf howl came once more above the rattle of the wheels.

The little cavalcade crossed the stream and climbed the opposite hill, the heavy-loaded wagons zigzagging upward with many rests. It was wholly dark when they gained the summit, and Tom Lockwood and his uncle went ahead carrying torches of fat pine that threw an uncertain yellow glow on the huge black boles of the trees.

Occasionally the eerie cry of the gray hunters would echo behind them in the hills, making the horses plunge nervously into their collars. At length the road seemed to become less rough, and all of a sudden it widened into a small clearing. In the middle of this dim space was a long, low shack of logs. A mongrel hound came out to bark at the weary horses and was instantly challenged by the dauntless Cub. A candle appeared at a window. Then, at the bearded man's hail, the door opened and a sullen-faced, shock-headed German emerged.

Ezra Lockwood greeted him civilly.

"Have you room for us and our horses for the night?" he asked.

The man scowled. "Yah," he grunted, "but you pay me first."

"Very well," said the traveler, quietly, "if so be that's your custom. First or last, it's nought to me." And he pulled out a rotund wallet.

When the man had his money he led the way toward the hostelry. Tom's uncle helped Mrs. Lockwood, a spirited little lady with flashing black eyes, to descend from one of the wagons, and they entered the tavern, while Tom assisted the drivers with their unharnessing. At last the animals were all in the crude shed that served for a stable, and the covers of the wagons made fast for the night.

Tom, still carrying his rifle, strode up to the inn door, and as he crossed the threshold he knew that there was something about the house he did not like. Certainly it was not the roughness of the place that he objected to. They had slept in some uncouth taverns on their way through the Pennsylvania wilderness. But a sort of vague uneasiness caused the tall young pioneer to look sharply about him as he sat down at the slab table. The room was bare enough. Log walls chinked with earth made three sides of it. Most of the fourth was taken up with a homemade brick oven and a fireplace in which a dirty kettle hung above the blaze. Some stools and blocks of wood stood about the table and these completed the furnishings of the place, though through the door of an adjoining room some tumbled bedding was visible.

Tom took all this in at a glance, and noted the surly bustle of the innkeeper and his wife as they placed a meal on the puncheon table. Then his eye came to rest on a ragged figure, squatting at one side of the fire. Above the mangy bearskin that wrapped its body, a pair of black eyes gleamed. Tom had seen many native people before, but never as dirty a specimen as this one.

He turned away to join his uncle and aunt at their supper. The food was of the coarsest, but their outdoor appetites enabled them to make away with it, and at length, the dishes being removed, their host sat down near them. His little eyes held a shrewd glint.

"You comin' from Philadelphy?" he remarked after a while.

Ezra Lockwood nodded. "Yes," he said, "we left the Schuylkill four weeks ago. Wanted to cross the mountains early so as to be ready to start from Pittsburgh with the first freshet."

There was silence for a while. Then the German man spoke again.

"Goin' for Ohio?" he asked, this time.

"Missouri," replied the bearded traveler.

"You got it friends oudt dere?" the innkeeper persisted.

"Yes," Ezra Lockwood explained. "A family named Coleman, old neighbors of ours, went over last year. From them we heard good report of the lands beyond the Mississippi and we are to join them out there in time to plant a few crops this season. The corn in that Missouri country, they say, grows as tall as a barn and bears six good ears to the stalk. I am myself a gunsmith by trade, and good rifles, I hear, are in much demand in those parts."

The German nodded his bristly head. "Yah, yah, so," he grunted, and Tom, watching him like a hawk, could have sworn he saw the German exchange a glance with the squatting native.

The gunsmith and his wife rose now and asked to be shown their sleeping place, for they had been on the trail since early morning. As there were but two bedrooms in the shack, Tom and the teamsters rolled themselves in their blankets on the floor of the kitchen. Candles were extinguished. The huge, maple log threw a faint, flickering light over the clay-daubed walls. Save for the occasional snapping of an ember on the hearth, the silence of the forest settled over the little inn in the clearing.

CHAPTER II

T HE SHARP CHILL of dawn penetrated the double thickness of Tom's blankets and he shivered and woke with a start. The wagoners still lay like logs on the floor. The fire had burned down to a few dull red coals in a heap of ash. Otherwise everything in the dim room seemed exactly as it had been the night before. And yet, half-awake as he was, Tom had a persistent feeling that something was different. His eye swept slowly about the place and in a flash he knew what it was he missed. The native man was not there. Some time in the night he must have slipped out noiselessly—and yet there was the heavy oak bar still in place across the door, and the window shutters were hooked from the inside. Here was a mystery that was to puzzle the boy many times in the days that followed.

The room grew lighter, and from somewhere back of the cabin came the loud crowing of a rooster. Tom shook the man next him awake.

"Come on, Brad," he said, "it's daylight. Time to get those horses fed, if we're going to make any twenty miles today."

The two hired men, Brad Bunker and Danny Flynn, grumbled once or twice, sleepily, then rose and staggered out to the tub of rainwater at the side of the shack. Tom had already broken the film of ice on its surface and was sousing his head and arms vigorously. He slatted the water off his black hair with his hand, drew the sleeve of his leather shirt once or twice across his face, and put his big coonskin cap back on his head jauntily. His toilet for the day was finished.

An hour later breakfast had been eaten, the horses hitched to the wagons, and the little caravan was forging forward on the road that ran like a dim aisle through the forest.

In that year of 1805 the way to the western country lay along the angles of a huge zigzag. From Philadelphia the Conestoga Road ran southwestward through Lancaster and York to the foot of the Alleghenies. There it split into several mountain trails which led in a general northwesterly direction to reunite at Pittsburgh. And from that bustling little port the waters of the Ohio carried the traveler southwestward once more until reaching the Mississippi.

It was along one of the rough tracks on the western slope of the Alleghenies that the Lockwoods' little wagon train was moving, that cold March day. The tavern where they had spent the night was one of a score of such ill-favored places, dotting the wilderness and ministering in a slipshod way to the needs of emigrants and freighters. Later in the season the roads would swarm with the big Conestoga wagons that plied between Philadelphia and the rapidly growing settlements of the upper Ohio Valley. And while these wagons jolted back and forth through the wilderness, along the same roads poured an ever-swelling stream of humanity—a stream that moved in only one direction—westward. All sorts of people made up the multitudes that choked in the swirling dust or struggled through the mud of the old Conestoga Road. The stout-hearted and God-fearing families of English and Scotch-Irish descent were not the only settlers who flocked over the mountain wall. A horde of dishonest men and gamblers from all along the seaboard were attracted to the new country, and they gathered in dissolute camps at every river landing and trading post.

It was a strange mixture of good and bad that populated the West of that generation. But fortunately for the history of our country the evildoers lived out their wild lives and disappeared, while the true pioneer farmers handed on their traditions to big families of sons and daughters.

The Lockwoods, like thousands of other households that moved westward in those years, were Eastern Pennsylvanians.

Tom's father and mother had been Quakers. Both had died in the great plague of yellow fever that swept Philadelphia in the summer of 1793, when Tom was still a little boy. He was taken by his Uncle Ezra to his home in Bucks County, and there among the farms and woods he had grown into a lad of seventeen, something over five-feet-ten in his moccasins, keen-eyed, self-reliant, and equally at home with an ax or a gun.

There were few boys of spirit at that period who did not have a secret desire to see the great, wild country beyond the blue Appalachian wall. Tom, you may be sure, was the first to urge his uncle to make the westward journey. And though Ezra Lockwood was comfortably settled and made a good living from his farm and his smithy, there remained in him a real pioneer's love of adventure. When an enthusiastic letter came back from his friends the Colemans, in Missouri, his mind was made up. He sold the Bucks County farm, purchased some good horses, packed his furniture and a supply of food in the big wagons, took his wife, his nephew and the two hired men who had been in his employ for years, and set out over the rutty winter roads.

The travelers had met trouble and adventure in the three hundred miles of wilderness they had traversed. Twice they were held up by snow in the hills and once, during an early spring thaw, the wagons were bogged in the mud for days. Wolves and an occasional panther prowled about their night camps.

But now that they were at last approaching Pittsburgh, circumstances seemed to favor them. The weather held clear and frosty, postponing the season of deep mud that they hoped to avoid. The horses continued in good condition, and as the hills grew lower they were able to make longer stages.

At length, on the morning of the fifth day after their stop at the inhospitable mountain tavern, they came down into the fair valley of the Monongahela and the trail merged with a broad highway along the riverbank. Following this road they came, in the late afternoon, to the little town built around old Fort Duquesne, that was already the gateway of the West.

On that sharp point of land between the rivers, Pittsburgh stood, a huddle of roughly-built houses, swarming upward from the shore. No pioneer settlement is beautiful. But the sunset light gave the place a mellow glow that made it loom up romantic and strange to Tom's eager eyes. He thrilled to a new sense of adventure as he rode down the wide dirt street, sitting very erect on his little white mare.

Ezra Lockwood had galloped ahead to find accommodation for the night. As the plodding wagons came abreast of the principal tavern, the gunsmith emerged, a frown of annoyance on his face.

"Not a room to be had, nor so much as a hitching place in the barns," he said. "Every house in Pittsburgh is full to over-flowing, they tell me."

They made inquiries of some of the many bystanders in front of the inn, and presently learned that other wagon trains like their own were camped on the bluff, half a mile up the Allegheny side. The weary horses were started once more and in a few minutes the travelers reached a small, grassy clearing above the town. Half a dozen tents and covered wagons stood in this open space, and here and there a supper fire was blazing. Tom dismounted and set to work at once gathering some dry wood, while Brad and Danny blanketed and fed the horses, and Ezra Lockwood made ready a sleeping place in one of the wagons.

By the time supper was over it had grown pitch-dark. Tom spread a tarpaulin between the wagon wheels and lay down under a bearskin, his long rifle on one side of him and the trusty little dog Cub on the other. In thirty seconds he had gone to sleep.

CHAPTER III

HALF AN HOUR after sunrise Pittsburgh was awake. The impression Tom had gained the night before, of a lazy backwoods village, changed at once as he walked down the river bank in the early morning. The sound of hammers, axes and saws rang loud on every hand. As far as Tom could see, along the shore, piles of timber and half-built hulls shouldered one another. At first glance it seemed as if every able-bodied man in the settlement had gone to work on the boats.

All this was easy to understand. With the spring freshets, which were nearly due, the travelers would begin to arrive in earnest. And hundreds—perhaps thousands—of flatboats would be needed to carry them down the river. The price of boats had climbed steadily from year to year. There was a huge profit to the builders, even though they were now forced to go some distance up the tributary streams for the big trees from which they hewed their lumber.

As Tom strolled along the bank, fascinated by the cheerful bustle of it all, a man began singing somewhere close by. It was a wild, jigging tune of the river that the boy never forgot:

"It's spring high water in Pittsburgh town,
    Oh, high, O-hi-o!
Lay her nose with the current an' let her run down,
    Oh, high, O-hi-o!
Down the big river, an' west by south.
To the Falls o' the Ohio an' the Wabash mouth—
For it's high water now, but there's gwineter be a drouth—
    Down on the O-hi-o!"

By one of the crude shipways Tom saw Ezra Lockwood in conversation with a tall fellow in a carpenter's apron. As he drew near, his uncle shook the man's hand heartily. Then he caught sight of Tom.

"It's all arranged, lad," he cried. "This good man will build us a keelboat, and have it ready for a start in three weeks' time!"

This was good news indeed, for the Lockwoods had heard stories of travelers who were forced to wait months for any sort of craft, in the height of the spring season. That Tom's uncle had happened to find an able shipwright just ready to start on a new boat was pure luck.

The boy stopped a while and watched the carpenter's businesslike preparations for laying the keel. Then he whistled to his dog and went on.

All manner of vessels were being built along the shore. The flat-bottomed, square-ended Kentucky boats, or "broadhorns," seemed to predominate. They were stout, simple affairs, hardly more than great boxes of hewn timber. Most of them were about forty feet long by sixteen wide, decked over, except for a square hatch near the bow. In the sides were openings for oars, and a port was cut in the stern to accommodate the long steering sweep. These craft could go only with the current. The oars helped in steering, but were powerless to propel the boat upstream.

Here and there a keelboat was being built, longer and narrower of beam than the flatboats, and though crude enough in construction, having something more of grace in its lines. These vessels, too, were steered by a clumsy oar, but they had walking planks, a foot or so in width, along either side, so that men with iron-shod poles could force them up against a fairly strong current. Most of them contained a roughly decked cabin, aft, but were open forward.

Tom, who had seen some shipbuilding of a different sort on the Delaware, was intensely interested in all this. He walked on around the point, and was just starting up the Monongahela side when he saw a crowd of men and boys standing about a small, improvised ring, in the shade of a ramshackle building. Shouts and shrill cheers came from this group, and Tom could catch an occasional glimpse, among the homespun legs, of something flashing to and fro. Curiosity drew him closer, and in a moment he was standing on the edge of the crowd, looking over a man's shoulder at his first cockfight.

Two gamecocks, a red and a gray, were sparring furiously in the center of the open space. Twice they danced back to opposite sides of the arena and hurtled at each other like feathered bullets. At the second of these encounters the gray bird leaped upward a fraction of a second before the other, and caught his adversary with a lightning-like stroke of the sharp steel gaff that pinned him through the neck just behind the head.

A lusty cheer was raised by the gray bird's backers and two of them rushed in to separate the birds as the red's fluttering ceased. Not without some quarreling the bets were paid.

A vague feeling of disgust filled Tom. He started off and had taken several strides up the bank when a loud hail caused him to stop.

"Whar ye goin', my buck?" shouted a heavy voice.

"Look'ee here, boy," said another man, as Tom turned, "we're rivermen an' we want a civil howdy-do from farmers an' lubbers."

Tom eyed the group without a word. He was about to go on about his business, but a glimpse of Cub made him pause once more. The dog was standing with feet braced, a ridge of stiff hair rising along his back. Out from the crowd of river toughs trotted a big black hound, hackles up and lips drawn back in a wicked snarl. Before Tom's hand could stay him, Cub had jumped forward to meet the enemy.

The rivermen laughed confidently. The black hound was half again as tall as Cub. Tom was silent but unworried, for he knew his dog. Cub was a mix, but a fighter clean through. His father had been a brindled pit bull, his mother a little brown

Irish terrier, and he had all the grim courage of the one, in addition to the alertness and speed of the other.

For the space of a second the two dogs stood shoulder to shoulder. Then the hound struck sidewise with a terrifying growl. His great white eyeteeth met with a clash just short of Cub's flank. The brown terrier had dodged, and now flew in for the big dog's throat. He missed but his teeth tore a gash in the black's foreleg. They rolled over in a gasping whirl, both trying for a grip, and for a moment none of the spectators could see what was happening. Then above the snarling din they heard a hideous yelp of pain that ended in a gurgle. The dust settled. On the ground writhed the black dog, while astride of him stood Cub, jaws clamped shut on his adversary's throat.

An angry clamor rose from the crowd while Tom stepped forward and pried his dog loose. After a gasp or two the hound got weakly to his feet and slunk off.

A tall, stockily built man with a heavy jaw and leering eyes took a stride toward Tom.

"Think yer dog kin fight, huh! How 'bout yerself? Here's the boss rough-an'-tumble fightin' boy o' the river jes' sp'ilin' fer to pull yer ears off. Come on thar, Andy!"

The men yelled with joy and a wiry youngster jumped out of the crowd, pulling off his jacket. He was not an ill-looking lad, Tom thought—redheaded and pug-nosed, with a pair of sparkling blue eyes full of devil-may-care mischief. He danced up to Tom, rolling up the sleeves of his butternut shirt as he came.

"Whadye think ye are—a hunter?" he cried, provocatively. "Been shootin' oysters, down to Philadelphy, I reckon! Look at the deerskin breeches on him!"

These sallies brought loud guffaws from the crowd, but Tom still stood quietly, his arms folded. He had no quarrel with this lad, half a head shorter and many pounds lighter than himself.

The redheaded boy flung his cap down on the ground, then stood on tiptoe and waved his arms like a crowing rooster.

"Cock-a-doodle-doo!" he cried shrilly. "Huh! I don't value you!"

This was fighting talk, as Tom well knew, but he made no move. The stocky riverman who had first spoken came forward angrily.

"See here, ye yaller pup—what are ye—a Quaker?" he taunted.

Tom reddened. His father had indeed been one of the peace-loving sect, and though he had fought under Washington he had tried to instill Quaker principles in his son.

"Well," sneered the big man, coming very close, "that fer you!" and he slapped Tom in the face with the back of his hand. The boy had passed the limit of his endurance. Like a flash his right fist shot out and landed solidly on the other's jaw. The fellow was caught unprepared and staggered backward half-bewildered. Then with a roar of rage he plunged at his younger antagonist.

The backwoodsmen of that day fought with as much ferocity and with as little science as animals. Biting, gouging, kicking and strangling were regarded as legitimate tactics. Now, as the big river bully charged in, he had sheer murder in his eyes. Fortunately Tom knew something of how to use his hands. Along the docks, in Philadelphia, he had seen the sailors fight, and he and his uncle had often boxed, for sport.

The boy was lithe and quick on his feet as a young panther. He jumped aside, tantalizingly avoiding the other's rush, then danced in close and jabbed the man in the face with a stiff left. The fellow blinked his eyes and groped wildly in the air with powerful hands. Tom, stepping easily out of reach, was gathering himself for another blow when his heel encountered an out cropping stone in the road, and he was flung off his balance. At that instant the riverman made a lunge and his grappling fingers caught Tom's arm. The boy struggled fiercely, but at close grips his older and heavier attacker was too much for him. He had seized Tom's right wrist with one hand and with the other he now grasped him by the throat. Wrench and twist as he would the boy could not shake off those vengeful fingers. He could no longer breathe. Desperately he drove his clenched left hand into the man's midriff—once—twice—and of a sudden the grip on his windpipe relaxed. Like many another bully, the riverman was fat at the waistline and out of condition. He grunted with pain, and dropped his hands to his belt instinctively.

Tom was cool again. In an instant he shifted his feet, measured the distance to the other's jaw, and whipped up his right fist in a clean uppercut that had all his vigorous young strength behind it. The man's arms dropped helplessly and he fell forward on his face.

The boy stood above him, tall and grim, breathing hard through his nose. All his fighting blood was up now.

"Any more?" he asked, in a voice that broke youthfully and made him angrier still. There was no answer from the rivermen. Only the fiery little redhead who had first challenged him came forward with real admiration in his eyes.

"Great jumpin' catamounts!" he gasped, "How'd ye do that?"

Sullen voices spoke from the group in the shadow of the building. "Shut yer trap, Andy!"—"Come back yere!" they growled.

The youngster—he could hardly have been more than sixteen—flushed to the roots of his carroty hair and swung toward his companions.

"Aw, I'll—" he began, but something seemed to check him, and he went slowly back to his place.

Tom had picked up his coonskin cap, which had fallen off in the struggle, and now he stalked away without a backward glance. At his heels trotted the blood-smeared but victorious Cub.

CHAPTER IV

Tom decided, wisely or not, to say nothing to his uncle about the affair with the rivermen. He knew that his own curiosity was to blame for it. After the repeated warnings he had heard from settlers and Conestoga freighters, he should have known enough to steer clear of the lawless waterfront gangs. He proceeded up the Monongahela bank for a mile or more, till he was out of sight of the town, and washed himself and his dog in a little stream, as best he could. They strolled casually into the wagon camp toward dinnertime, and Tom was relieved to find everyone too busy to ask questions. In the afternoon he helped the hired men erect a temporary shelter of poles and brush, which would serve to keep the horses out of the weather until Ezra Lockwood could find a purchaser for them. Part of the goods in one of the wagons had been removed and piled on the ground under a tarpaulin, to give Mrs. Lockwood roomier sleeping quarters, and it fell to Tom's lot to guard this heap of material. He was nothing loath, for sleeping out had always had a fascination for him. He liked to lie, on a clear night, and watch the slow march of the armies of the stars. So it was, that long after the campfire had sunk to a red mass of coals Tom remained wide awake, his mind ranging the broad fields of the sky.

A sudden movement on the part of Cub, who had been lying beside him, brought the boy back to earth. The dog had jumped up and was standing with cocked ears, looking toward the edge of the clearing. A slow lifting of the hair along his spine and a faint rumble in his throat warned his owner to get ready for something. Tom sat up silently and put fresh priming in the pan of his rifle. His eyes, always exceptionally keen, were wholly accustomed to the dark, for he had not been asleep. He knew that though Cub's hearing was more acute than his own, he could see at least as well as the dog, and he watched intently the rim of the forest toward which the scarred brown head was turned. For minutes on end the two kept up their vigil. Then as if by magic, from the ground a dozen yards away a figure rose.

Cub's growl changed to a threatening snarl and he would have leaped forward had not Tom's hand caught him by the scruff. The long rifle was rested across the boy's knee and his forefinger was on the trigger.

"Stand still or I'll fire," he said steadily.

"Wait—want to talk to ye!" a stifled voice whispered.

"Who are you?" asked Tom.

"Andy—Andy Warren, the feller that was agoin' to fight you," answered the voice.

Tom lowered the muzzle of his gun. "All right," he said, "come on."

He got to his feet and subdued the still belligerent Cub with a short command. The other lad drew near, and Tom could see, even in the starlight, that he must have been crawling through briers and underbrush. His clothes were torn and his face scratched and he was hatless.

"If they ever git holt o' me, they'll sure kill me," he muttered, as he came close.

Tom was watching warily for a trap of some sort, but he knew when he heard the other's voice and saw the shiver with which he glanced over his shoulder, that this was genuine fear. Impulsively his heart went out to the boy.

"Tell me about it," he said.

They sat down with their backs against the pile of freight, and Andy began.

"Guess ye didn't know who it was ye laid out, this mornin', did ye? Well, it was Black Carnahan," his voice sank to a whisper of real terror, "Black Carnahan of the Wilson Gang!"

This conveyed nothing to Tom. He waited.

"He's the dirtiest fighter on the hull river," Andy explained. "When he gits through with a feller, he's gen'ally dead. Wal, when Black come to, arter you hit him, he was ravin' an' r'arin'. Some sneak tolt him I'd hollered fer you to win, an' he started arter me. Twice he most got me, too, but I dodged an' run into the woods, an' I been hidin' out all day.

"Ye know," Andy paused with a sort of awkward shyness, "ye know I thought I could fight, myself. I've walloped the tar out'n most every boy on the river, but I never seen no sich a scrapper as you—no, siree! You're the yaller flower o' the forest! An'—an' say—could ye take me down the river?"

Tom was startled by the request, but he had liked this boy from the start.

"I reckon maybe so," he said. "Tell me though—how'd you come to get in with that crew?"

"When I was jest a little tyke," replied Andy, "my pappy was a pilot, down't the Falls o' the Ohio. He got drownded shootin' the rips, an' there wa'n't no one to take keer o' me. So some o' the rivermen begun to let me sleep an' eat aboard o' their boats. They was a bad lot— workin' in cahoots with Jericho Wilson an' his Cave Gang—you must 'a' heerd o' them—an' stealin' boats whenever they got a chanct. I been tryin' to git free of 'em for years, but they made much o' me, an' used to pick fights with other boys, so's they could bet their money on me. But I'm sick of it. I'd a heap sight rather go with you. I got to git away from here now, but I could hide out in the woods, below Wheelin', an' git aboard when you come down the river. They's a cove with some big sycamore trees on the bank, maybe five miles down from Wheelin' on the Virginia side. Then you could put your boat in as you went down, an' I'd be waitin' fer ye—"

He broke off, his eyes fixed eagerly on Tom's face.

The taller boy had made up his mind. "I believe you mean what you say," he answered, "and I think I can make Uncle Ezra believe it, too. Jiminy, won't we have sport, though! I've been wishing there was another boy my age to go down with us. Say—you can shoot, can't you? You'll need a gun if you're going to cross over to Wheeling through the woods. Here, I've got two rifles. You take this one. And here's some powder and bullets. Got your own flint an' steel, I reckon?"

"Got everything!" said Andy. "An' say—I'll take plumb good keer o' that rifle, too. Ain't she a beauty!"

"It's a Lockwood gun," answered Tom proudly. "They don't come any better. I reamed that one, and set her sights, myself."

The two boys went together to the edge of the clearing.

"Watch out fer that gang o' Carnahan's," said Andy. "I don't cal'late they'd tetch ye here in the town, but down the river they might."

"Right," Tom answered. "Good luck to you, Andy. In three weeks, barring accidents, we'll put in for you at Sycamore Cove."

The redheaded lad gave him a solid grip of the hand and vanished silently into the woods.

Tom returned to his blankets and lay for a while wriggling with joy as he thought of this newfound comradeship and all that it would mean to him in his voyage of adventure. Then he went to sleep, leaving the watchful Cub on guard.

The next morning dawned clear and balmy—a true early spring day. As soon as the chores were done and breakfast eaten, Tom went to his uncle and told him in a straightforward way of his visit from the orphaned river lad on the previous evening. As he had expected, Ezra Lockwood generously approved his nephew's course in the matter.

"The boy will make a good companion for you, and an extra hand who knows the river will be a help to all of us," he said.

The two were about to start down the shore in the direction of the boatyards, when a man entered the clearing and came towards them with a strange, agile sort of limp, that carried him rapidly over the ground. Patched blue cloth breeches and jacket covered his large, gaunt frame, and a felt hat was cocked on the side of his head and pulled down over one ear. As he approached, his leather-like face broke into a wrinkling smile. His eyes, of a peculiar sharp gray, darted from Ezra to Tom and back again.

"Howdy, folks," he said, in a pleasant voice. "Mr. Lockwood, ain't it? I been a-wonderin' how soon you'd come over the mountains. My name's Rogers—Jake Rogers—an' I'm a reg'lar river pilot. Last year I took three different boatloads o' travelers down. Le's see, you're friends o' the Colemans, ain't you?"

"Yes, indeed," said Tom's uncle, a trifle surprised. "Do you know them?"

"Know 'em!" Rogers fairly shouted, "Know 'em, I should say I do! Why, I took their boat all the way to St. Louis, an' if I do say it as shouldn't, we had a fine v'yage. The Colemans was so pleased with the way I steered, they said they sure hoped I'd be free fer a job when their friends the Lockwoods come over. Jes' so happened I heerd down to the tavern that ye'd pulled in, an' I come up to see if ye hed a pilot yet."

"Well, well!" said Ezra. "I've been wondering where I was to get a good steersman. The town's full of lazy rogues that I wouldn't trust. This is luck, sure enough! Now, if the shipwright is as good as his word, we'll be ready to start in three weeks' time. Would that suit you, Mr. Rogers?"

The lame riverman replied heartily that the date would fit

in perfectly with his plans. "As for pay," he laughed, "don't let that fret ye none! I'm not one o' these graspin' loafers. I sail the river becus I like it. Whatever ye want to give me, that'll suit ol' Jake."

And after a few more reassurances of this sort, the man limped off down the bank, waving a friendly farewell.

Ezra turned to Tom with a smile. "That's another piece of luck, lad," he said. "Good pilots are rare, they say. This fellow will fill the bill splendidly, and it's a big relief to me to find him, I can tell you."

CHAPTER V

THE DAYS SPED FAST, and every sunset saw the keelboat nearer completion. At last she was given a coat of pitch, and the boat-builder announced that within two days she would be ready to launch. The Lockwoods, meanwhile, had finished their preparations for the start. The big draft horses had been sold to a freighter for a good price, and even after paying for his boat Ezra Lockwood's bags contained several thousand dollars—a considerably larger sum than most travelers carried in those days. Tom felt badly at having to part with the little Pocono mare, but he had known from the beginning that it must be so, and at least he was able to make sure that she went to a good home.

The rivers had been rising as the snow melted in the hills, and now the freshet was nearing its height. Buds were opening on the hardwood trees, and the April sun shone warmly down the length of the great valley. Daily now the muddy, creaking wagons came out of the forest, on the Conestoga Road. And daily the boats of traders and emigrants swung free from the piers and sailed away downstream. The spring exodus had begun.

It was just twenty days after their first sight of Pittsburgh that the Lockwoods stowed their cargo of household goods, gunsmith's tools and provisions aboard the good ship *Phoebe Ann*—she was named after Tom's aunt—and waited for sunrise to start their voyage. Tom spent that last night on board, guarding the craft and its valuable freight. At daylight he was roused by a hail from the dock, and was relieved to see the tall, bony figure of their pilot standing there. Nothing had been heard of him since the day of his first appearance at the clearing and Tom knew that his uncle had felt some concern lest the man should fail to be on hand.

"Wal, sonny," cried Rogers, jovially, "sho' is a day, ain't it! Had breakfast yet? I got a fire up the bank here, an' some deer's meat a-cookin'."

The boy jumped ashore with alacrity, for the cold air of dawn had given him a keen appetite. As they mounted the bank together Tom was surprised once more at the rapid ease of the man's limping stride. He might have been made of whalebone and rawhide for there seemed to be no flesh on his spare frame.

They crouched beside the smoking venison and fell to with knives and fingers. After the first few wolfish mouthfuls, Rogers turned to the little heap of his belongings which lay by the fire and drew out a tall, slender stone bottle. He took a long pull, smacked his lips and proffered the jug to Tom, who smilingly refused it. He knew something of Pittsburgh whiskey.

Now that the pilot's hunger was appeased and his tongue somewhat loosened, he began to talk. Hair-raising tales of the Ohio, seasoned with strange river oaths, poured from him in a flood. Tom listened and at the same time he watched. There was something disturbing to him in the odd gleam of the man's eyes and the flash of his big yellow teeth. And he could not help speculating on the strange angle of the felt hat, which, as before, was pulled down on the left side so far that it almost brushed Rogers' shoulder.

At length Mr. and Mrs. Lockwood appeared on the dock, below, and the riverman jumped to his feet. As he picked up his duffel bag, a bundle of striped fur at the end of a chain emerged, spitting, from behind it.

"Ha-ha!" laughed Rogers. "I clean fergot to make ye 'quainted with this little feller. Gin'ral Wayne his name is, an' he's the champeen fightin' coon o' the valley. We'll hev to keep him 'way from thet dog o' yourn, or the Gin'ral's liable to bite him in two!" And one side of the leathery face wrinkled in a wink.

The *Phoebe Ann's* passengers were soon aboard, and without further preliminaries the moorings were cast off. A strong swing on the steering oar, as she caught the current, sent the craft far out into midstream. A little cheer went up from the boatbuilders along the shore. At last the travelers had begun the long, final stage of their westward journey.

Tom felt a huge exhilaration as the prow of the keelboat shot past the lower point of the town, and into the Ohio itself. Astern of them the morning sun glinted on the mile-wide swirl of waters. Ahead, the mighty curves of the river unfolded themselves steadily, in an ever changing prospect.

The muddy current ran bank high between shores heavily wooded with oaks and maples and great, straight-stemmed tulip trees. The speed they made astonished Tom at first. Easily and without effort, the long craft slipped downstream at a uniform six miles an hour. As he watched the forests glide past, the boy could not help thinking of the weary plodding it had cost to come thus far. He had not realized, before, what an advantage the great water highway held over land travel. Then, too, the distances that had to be traversed! Though they seemed to be fairly flying westward, he knew that few boats reached the Mississippi in less than twenty days. Jake Rogers lolled on the sun-warmed deck, astern, one elbow flung over the steering sweep. He had taken off his coat and rolled up the sleeves of his faded woolen shirt, disclosing lean, brown forearms, as hard and corded as an ironwood sapling. His ancient hat, however, still sat rakishly on his head. The man nodded merrily, when Tom went aft to join him, early in the afternoon.

"Yes, sir, sonny," he cried, "ye're on the river now, sho 'nough! Come back to hev a parley with ol' Jake, eh?" He paused long enough to spit over his shoulder, then pointed a bony forefinger toward the north bank.

"Boy," he said, his voice sinking to a serious and confidential tone, "boy, on that p'int yonder, I seen four men killed once— killed an' sculped. Thirty year ago, 'twas, 'fore Colonel Clark took Cahokia. I dove under the boat, that time, an' swum clean acrost the river in the dark, with them natives arter me in canoes. Ho, hum! I been up an' down this river! Yes, siree!" And he swung into the odd, jigging chorus of a river song, slapping his hand on the deck to keep time.

Before sunset they ran in and moored their boat on the Virginia shore, opposite the Steubenville settlement. A cooking fire was built on the bank. After supper the party sat about the blaze for a while, then returned to the boat and slumbered soundly, for the sun and wind on the river had made them all sleepy.

Daylight woke them, and as soon as breakfast had been eaten they resumed their voyage.

Tom knew that the town of Wheeling was not many miles below, and mindful of Andy Warren, he watched for the place expectantly. About noon they saw log and brick houses on the left shore, going up steeply from the river. This was a different sort of town from Pittsburgh. No busy boatyards were visible, but they caught distinctly the sound of whoops and cheers, and along the high street a crowd of men could be seen.

"Thar they go!" shouted Rogers, pointing, excitedly. As he spoke, Tom caught sight of two men on horseback, flying down the dirt road at a dead run. More cheers resounded, as the riders slowed up beyond the last scattering of houses.

"That's Wheelin' fer ye!" chuckled Jake. "Don't do nothin' thar all day long but race hosses!"

The keelboat sped on, out of sight of the town, and now Tom stood eagerly by the port bulwark and scanned the river below. After half an hour or so he saw what he was looking for—an inward curving bay in the southern shore,

"There's the place, Uncle Ezra!" he called.

"Right," answered his uncle. "Put in for that cove, below there, Rogers."

The gaunt steersman appeared not to hear.

"Bear over to the left there, I say!" Ezra Lockwood shouted. "You'll be too far down if you don't hurry!"

Rogers looked surprised. "That 'ere cove!" he said, "That ain't no fit place to land—there's rocks in the river, 'long here."

The bearded gunsmith took a stride in Rogers' direction. "Put that helm over at once," he ordered sharply. "We'll chance the rocks."

With a somewhat grudging air, the pilot swung his oar at last, and the nose of the boat turned toward the cove. They neared the shore rapidly. The rocks, if any existed, did not interfere with their progress, and in a few moments Tom had clambered up the steep bank, under the giant sycamores. He had half expected Andy to be waiting on the shore, but there was no sign of him among the trees, nor did any sound but the chattering of squirrels answer Tom's call. There was a gloominess about the place that was depressing. The boy waited a few minutes, then shouted once more. Finally he turned back to the bank, in disappointment, and started climbing down by the root of a large beech tree. Casually his glance swept upward and he gave a startled exclamation. There on the trunk, not two feet above his head, were odd characters, freshly carved in the bark. He drew himself up on a level with the blaze and examined it carefully. At the left was a crudely shaped arrowhead, pointing downward. Next came four rough circles. The row of symbols was completed on the right by a deep slit in the bark, into which a splinter of wood had been driven. Peering closer, Tom saw a wisp of something bright-colored pinned by this wedge. It was a tiny lock of vivid red hair.

"Andy's!" he cried, and was just about to pluck the splinter from the crevice when something sang past his head, and at the same instant the crack of a rifle was heard.

"Quick, Tom!" shouted his uncle, "get back aboard here!"

But the boy had already gained the afterdeck in one long leap. "Shove off!" he cried, and within a dozen seconds the boat was once more shooting down the river.

CHAPTER VI

THE LANDING AT SYCAMORE COVE, and Tom's futile search there for Andy, had consumed the best part of an hour. It was past three o'clock in the afternoon when the Pennsylvanians pushed off from shore with the sound of the rifle shot ringing in their ears. Tom found his uncle waiting for him in the little cabin of the keelboat. There were stern lines about his bearded mouth.

"See here, lad," he said, as Tom entered, "I hope you're satisfied now. The rascals set a pretty trap for you and into it you tumbled, like a bear into a honeypot. 'Twas luck alone that we were not all killed!"

Tom flushed. "No, Uncle," he said, "I still think Andy was honest. If you'd seen him, you would, too—"

"Honest!" Ezra Lockwood snorted. "Perhaps that shot was fired in fun, then? The bullet went through the planking here, not a yard from my bunk!"

The boy shook his head doggedly. "Wait, Uncle Ezra," said he. "Just before they fired I found a sign from Andy on a tree, there by the water. An arrow pointing down, then four circles, sort of, and a bit of his own red hair, stuck in a cleft. I've figured it out and it all seems plain to me. What I think he meant to tell me is that he'll be waiting four days further down the river. Likely that cove is a landing place for these outlaws, and some of them came there so he didn't dare stay."

"Huh!" replied his uncle. "Well, we'll have no more running ashore and risking our necks for the scamp, at any rate. To tell you the truth, I think he and his gang no better than a crew of pirates."

Tom swallowed his feelings and climbed to the afterdeck, where he joined Jake Rogers. The lanky helmsman was whistling with the greatest cheerfulness.

"Wal, Tommy," he chuckled, "I told ye no good'd come o' goin' ashore in that forsaken cove. Better take ol' Jake's advice arter this—*hum-te-tum-tum-teedle-deedle-tum-te-teedle-dee*—" and he swung into the chorus of one of his endless boatman's songs.

The sun sank lower and gilded the reaches of the river, ahead. A few more miles they slipped downward, then put in for a landing. Their camp was on the Ohio shore this time.

"Bank ain't so steep. More trees to tie to," explained Rogers.

It was a wild place, and Tom, lying awake forward, where he slept with Bunker and Flynn, twice heard the scream of a catamount, hunting in the woods far away. The sound made him shift uneasily in his blankets, for it fitted in with his thoughts. He wondered if Andy had reached the new rendezvous, four days down the river, or if the lad was even now lying by a tiny fire somewhere in that vast wilderness between. The faint, far-off screech of the panther came again, and Tom shivered as he fell asleep.

It was broad daylight when Brad Bunker shook him awake. Already the boat was in motion and the crew had eaten breakfast. Tom got a bite for himself and took up his station in the bow where he could watch the panorama of the river.

"We're comin' into the Long Reach, now," sang out Rogers from his post at the stern. Eighteen miles, she is, straight— 'thout a curve. Islands in the middle. Main channel's on the right."

Tom, looking ahead, saw a great sweep of water opening out before them. The river stretched away southward as far as the eye could see. It was dinnertime before the keelboat had floated through the lower end of the Long Reach. As if to make up for its good behavior, the Ohio now twisted into sharp oxbow curves, one after another, that continued for a number of miles. The current switched from side to side of the river, running deep and swift along the outer bank at every bend, and Jake Rogers, by the stern oar, was kept on the alert to hold the craft in the full sweep of the channel. Several times even his dexterous steering was barely successful in keeping the boat out of the angry eddies and whirlpools that edged the current.

They covered more than twenty miles of this wild part of the river in a scant three hours. The sun was still fairly high when the prow of the keelboat swept around a great point, and Tom, posted as a lookout, cried that he saw a broad stream running into the Ohio from the North.

"The Muskingum, it must be," replied Ezra Lockwood. "We'd best put in and spend the night at the Marietta settlement, for I want to buy powder and fish lines."

The boat was run closer to the right bank, and in a few moments lay moored with several other craft, to the one crude dock that formed the little town's waterfront.

As soon as the ropes were made fast, Tom took his rifle, called to Cub, who was eager to stretch his legs on shore, and walked with his uncle up the main street of the settlement. There seemed to be a considerable crowd of people in and about the log house which served as a general store. Among them, as Tom approached, he noticed at least a score of tall men dressed in buckskin tops and fringed breeches like his own. Most of them wore the customary coon-and-squirrelskin caps, but one great, broad-shouldered fellow had adorned himself with a headgear of bearskin, and another had on a cap of wolf's fur with the ugly black snout and inch-long eyeteeth grinning wickedly above his keen, tanned face. This man, slighter of build than some of his fellows, but with an erect, soldierly carriage, was bartering furs for flour and pork, as the Lockwoods entered. While they stood waiting for the storekeeper to be free, the huge man with the cap of bearskin came up, grinning in friendly fashion.

"Howdy, trav'lers," he said. "Ye got started early, didn't ye? We aim to push off 'fore the rush starts, too. How fur ye goin'?"

"Missouri," replied Tom. "Where are you bound?"

"We're headed that way, too," said the giant, "only we're a-goin' up the Missouri River, into the beaver country—trappin'. We're long hunters from the upper Muskingum. Most of us was raised round here from children. But it's gittin' too full o' folks, up the river, thar." His face clouded and he shook his head. "Two new settlements up thar, 'thin thirty miles of each other! Dunno what this here country's a-comin' to."

There was real distress in the man's face, but it cleared, after a moment. "Wal, we're a-goin' on West, whar the crowds won't spile the huntin'," he said, more cheerfully. "That 'ar feller," his voice dropped, respectfully, and he nodded toward the man with the wolf's head on his cap, "that's Buckeye Ben Chandler. Call him that 'cause he kin shoot a deer through the eye, every time. Ben's the leader o' this here expedition. Two keelboats an' thirty men, we've got."

The Muskingum men's chief had now finished his negotiations with the storekeeper and Ezra Lockwood went over to make his purchases.

"Here, Ben," called Tom's big friend, "here's a youngster that'll be a woodsman, some day. He's goin' to Missouri, too."

The face under the wolf's teeth smiled, as Buckeye Ben drew near. He looked at Tom with searching gray eyes.

"Yes," he said at length, "looks like a real 'long hunter.'" His eye fell upon the rifle in the crook of Tom's arm, and he took a step nearer. "That's a good gun, boy," he nodded. "Lockwood make, ain't it?"

"My uncle made it," said Tom, proudly. "He's Ezra Lockwood."

"You don't say!" exclaimed the hunter, eagerly. "Why, I been carryin' one o' his rifles for years, an' there ain't no truer shootin' gun 'twixt here an' the Mississip' than ol' Sal, is ther', B'ar?"

He addressed the last question to the big man beside him.

"She sure is a nice shooter," the latter replied with a grin, "but—wal, ye know I've allus kinder stood up fer my ol' Jonathan Ames, here—"

"Come outside, then—come outside, an' I'll prove that my rifle kin spit lead further an' straighter'n any gun that ever come out o' New England!"

Chandler started toward the door, followed by half a dozen cheering hunters. "Come on, boys," someone called, "Buckeye Ben an' B'ar Hanson's goin' to shoot." The huge fellow in the bearskin cap winked at Tom. "Jes' said it to rile him," he chuckled. "Now ye'll see some fun." And he went to join the group outside.

Two of the hunters were already pacing off a distance. They stopped and one shouted back, "Here's two hundred."

"Make it two hundred an' fifty," answered Buckeye Ben promptly.

Tom watched them add fifty more yards to the range, then set up a piece of shingle against a tree. It was a nearly rectangular bit of wood, perhaps eight inches high by six across. At that distance it was not much more than visible.

"All right, B'ar, go ahead," said Chandler. The big woodsman had been loading his rifle with considerable care. Now he braced his feet and leveled the weapon, taking a long sight. When at last he fired they saw the shingle jump a little, then fall back, apparently untouched.

"Ol' Jonathan ain't feelin' very stout today, is he?" laughed Buckeye Ben, as he raised his own rifle, slowly. At the instant it reached the level of the shoulder, he fired. The target was split cleanly from top to bottom, but remained in position against the tree, its two halves separated by an inch or less. A loud yell went up from the assembled hunters. "That's ol' Sal fer ye!" "Good boy, Ben!" "Right betwixt the ears!"

Buckeye Ben turned toward Tom. "Try a shot yerself, son," he said kindly.

The boy flushed red with embarrassment under his tan, then stepped out boldly and took his position with feet spread, at right angles to the target. It was fortunate, he thought, that he had cleaned the rifle and loaded it that afternoon, using a heavy powder charge to carry far over the water if necessary. He paused a second to feel the wind, then lifted the barrel till the knife-like front sight came into view in the carefully filed notch of the rear bar. He found the white speck of the shingle, allowed for wind and distance, and pulled the trigger with a steady, even pressure that he had learned by long practice.

With the crash of the discharge all looked toward the target, but this time there was no resultant shattering of the wood.

Chandler smiled, sympathetically. "That's pretty fur fer any gun to shoot straight," he was saying, when a hail came from one of the men near the target. "Square between 'em!" the fellow called. "Couple o' inches above your'n, Ben!"

"Wal, I snum!" chorused the woodsmen. "Good shootin', thar, lad!" And B'ar Hanson smote Tom a powerful buffet between the shoulders.

"You'll do, boy!" he shouted. "If that had been a pa'tridge or a squirrel, you'd ha' got it."

Tom was anxious to escape from the rough flattery of the crowd of hunters, and seeing his uncle leaving the store, he started toward the dock, inviting the good-natured giant, Hanson, to go with him,

"Buckeye, he's the best shot above the Falls," explained the Muskingum man, as they went down the street. "He's a Kaintuck hunter, like ol' Danny Boone, an' Simon Kenton, an' they kin all drive a shoe peg with their rifles.

"That's your keelboat, is she? Nice, trim lookin' boat. Ain't you a leetle might skeert, though, goin' down with only three-four fightin' hands? Better wait a few days an' go down 'long of us."

Tom laughed. "Guess we'll get through all right," he said. "Four of us are good shots, an' this dog here's better'n two men. Then we've got a first-class riverman for pilot." He looked around for Jake Rogers but the lean steersman was nowhere to be seen.

"What makes you think we ought to go easy?" Tom pursued.

"That Wilson gang, below the Wabash, got mighty pesky 'fore the season was over, last fall," answered the big woodsman, with a frown. "We heard o' their work, way up on the Muskingum. That 'ar 'Jericho,' as they call him, sort o' collects all the mean scum an' trash from the hull river—some says they's a hundred of 'em now, jes' boozin' an' livin' off the travelers that comes down. Wish they'd tackle these boats of ourn, once! Only they don't fool much with hunters. We're too much like a razorback hog. The meat on our bones ain't wuth the ruction it takes to git it."

Dusk had begun to fall now, and the water ran past, gloomy and dark. Tom was looking across toward the Virginia shore, when his eye chanced to fall on a black speck, coming rapidly down with the current. It grew larger as it approached, and the force of the stream drove it nearer and nearer to the Ohio bank.

"Look there," said Tom, "in the big river. It's a canoe, isn't it?"

"Sure 'nough!" Hanson exclaimed. "Dugout, it looks like."

The little craft drew close and they could see a man kneeling amidships, plying his paddle vigorously, his head bent low. Suddenly Tom gave a start. The man's face had been turned in their direction for an instant, and the dark, coarse features of a native had been visible. Something about the slouched shoulders and matted hair reminded Tom of the night in the mountain inn, and the squatting figure by the fire that had disappeared before dawn. In that second the impression came vividly into Tom's mind that the native in the canoe was the same man.

Even as they watched, the tiny boat shot past the settlement, and was soon far downstream. Then an odd thing happened. When the canoe had reached a point perhaps a quarter of a mile below the town, Tom and his companion saw the paddle flash in the air and remain poised for several seconds, as if in signal to someone on shore. A moment later the craft had passed from sight.

The big New Englander, B'ar Hanson, stayed for supper at the Lockwoods' boat, then bade them a hearty farewell and returned to the hunters' camp, farther up the Muskingum shore.

Tom had wrapped himself in his blankets when he heard a step that rattled the gravel on the bank. His uncle's voice sounded. "Hello—that you, Rogers?" he asked.

"I'm that same," came the low, chuckling response of the pilot. "Jes' been fer a leetle stroll on the shore. Useter know a feller 'long the bank here a ways."

And Tom, wondering whether the riverman's stroll had taken him up the shore or down, finally fell asleep.

CHAPTER VII

THE MORNING DAWNED clear and bright, as the travelers
pushed off from the Marietta dock. So far, at least, the spring
weather had been unusually kind to them. According to the
genial Jake Rogers, a succession of half a dozen fair days was
almost unheard of on the river in April.

Ezra Lockwood had bought several fish lines and a supply
of hooks, and Tom spent most of the day fishing over the side
as they drifted down the river. About the middle of the morning the boat passed the mouth of the Little Kanawha, and
soon after, coming around a bend, they caught a glimpse of
Blennerhasset's "Castle" as the pilot called it, standing among
great trees on an island. The sight of that fine house with its
gardens, set in the midst of the wilderness, interested Tom by
its strangeness, though he had no way of knowing that the
name of the poor misguided gentleman who built it would be
written romantically into the history of his country. After a
curious glance or two he turned back to his fishing. Perch and
catfish were rising hungrily to the lure of his salt-pork bait,
and he soon had all the fish that the passengers and crew of
the *Phoebe Ann* could eat.

Two more days of perfect weather followed, and the travelers continued their steady progress down the river, making an easy fifty or sixty miles between sunrise and dark. Their landings were made, as a rule, on the southern shore, and at regular mooring places, where the bank was favorable for them. From his talks with Rogers, Tom had found out that these landing spots were known to all the pilots and nearly always used by boats descending the river. Thus, when a riverman said "two days downstream" he indicated a particular point on the bank, perhaps a hundred miles below.

Remembering Andy's message, carved on the beech trunk, Tom looked forward to the fourth night's landing with a growing hope that he would see his young friend.

Ezra Lockwood appeared stubbornly convinced that Andy had tried to trick them, and once, during the fourth day's cruise, he repeated to Tom his stern warning against going ashore to search for the redheaded lad. "We'll all sleep aboard, tonight," he said, "and we'd best have extra guns loaded, too. Rogers says the outlaws are too great of cowards to attack us openly, but it can do no harm to be ready."

Tom cleaned the rifles and loaded them without a word. At sunset the keelboat swung in toward the Kentucky shore, a dozen miles above the Scioto, and Flynn and Bunker had soon made a mooring rope fast to a big tree near the water. By Ezra Lockwood's orders, the shore fire was doused as soon as supper was finished, and all turned in on the planks of the boat. Jake Rogers took the first watch, while Tom was to have the second. Lying in his blankets near the bow, the young Pennsylvanian found himself too restless for slumber. He lay wide awake, his muscles tense, his ears strained to catch the slightest sound.

Aft on the deck of the cabin, he could see the gaunt silhouette of the steersman, black against the night sky. Rogers spat over the rail, and occasionally hummed one of his numberless river ditties under his breath. Suddenly the man stood up, rifle in hand.

"Who's that?" he asked, sharply. There was no answer but a faint splash in the water. For a moment Rogers stood motionless, his rifle half-raised. Then he settled back to his former comfortable position. "Nothin' but a muskrat, I reckon," be muttered.

For another hour Tom lay waiting. Then the pilot rose with a yawn and a stretch and came forward. He poked the boy's ribs with his toe. "Time fer you to stand watch," he grunted.

Ten minutes later, Tom was ensconced on the afterdeck, and the low, even snoring that came from the bow announced that Rogers was deep in sleep. Tom lifted himself softly, and looked over the side into the narrow lane of black water that separated them from the shore. Even as he did so, a whisper came out of the dark.

"Give me a hand up," said Andy's voice. Leaning far over, Tom felt fingers clutch his own, and a moment later he pulled the dripping figure of the riverboy to the deck beside him. Andy's teeth chattered with cold, and at first he could hardly speak.

"I—I—I started to come aboard b-before," he managed, at last, "only I g-got a sight o' that feller's face when he was leaning over, an' seen how his hat was pulled down on the side." His voice dropped once more to a whisper of pure terror. "Do you know who that is?" he said.

Tom shook his head in amazement. "Who?" he asked.

"That man," Andy answered, "is Earless Jake Rogers. He got his left ear bit off in a fight at the Falls o' the Ohio, years ago. He's one o' the meanest scrappers on the river, an'," Andy's whisper became almost inaudible, "he's Jericho Wilson's right-hand man!"

CHAPTER VIII

Tom sat with his eyes fixed on Andy's face, and his mouth open in astonishment.

"You mean," he gasped, "that Jake Rogers—our guide—is an outlaw—one of the river pirates?"

"That's jest what I mean," replied the smaller boy. "He's not only one of 'em, but one o' the worst. I seen him stick a knife clean through a feller, up at Chillicothe, onct, and when he's drunk he don't keer fer man nor devil. Br-r-r-r—got a blanket I could wrop up in?"

Tom went silently below and brought up a bearskin, which the shivering Andy threw over his shoulders. When the boy's teeth no longer chattered he began in a whisper to tell the story of his adventures.

"I got acrost to Wheelin' all right," he said. "Shot a turkey an' et that fer three days. Then I fixed me up a little shack in the woods, just uphill from the Sycamore cove. I was havin' a fine time there, all by my lonesome, when one day, a week 'fore you was due, a flatboat full o' men come to shore. I didn't see 'em till they was right on top o' me. Fust thing I know I heard a voice say, 'Hello, thar's Andy!' an' here come a feller named Bije Carey, that used to know me downriver. Him an' his crowd o' roughs had jest left Wheelin' bound fer Cincinnati. That cove's a sort o' hangout fer 'em. 'Course they didn't know 'bout my runnin' away from Black Carnahan, but they made me come aboard with 'em. I figgered I could meet you down here farther, so I cut them marks on the tree, while we was all settin' around on the bank. You found 'em, didn't you?"

"Yes," said Tom. "I thought we'd meet you here. But how'd you get away from their boat?"

"Swum," answered Andy, laconically. "Jumped overboard opposite the p'int, up yonder. Got my rifle a leetle wet an' so I didn't have nothin' to eat fer a day, but since then I been gettin' on fine.

"Now, Tom, what do you figger this man Rogers is doin' aboard your boat? He must be up to some game or other, 'cause he ain't no reg'lar pilot—no more'n I be. Ye'd better tell yer uncle, an' we'll all watch him. I'd ruther hev a rattlesnake aboard, myself."

Tom considered a moment. "I'll tell Uncle." he replied, "though he's mightily set in his opinions and he thinks a heap of Rogers as a pilot. But you and I can keep our eye on him. I believe he's up to something, myself. I can remember a lot of things he's done that seemed a little odd. You'll have to keep hid, though. If he saw you, he'd know we were on to him."

It was not until the small hours of the morning that the boys completed their plans. Then Tom stowed his friend away in a snug nest behind some bales of goods in the hold, and after giving him a ration of hardtack, roused Brad Bunker to take the morning watch.

The young Pennsylvanian slept no more that night. As he went forward to his blankets, he glanced down at the snoring pilot. Rogers' hat had fallen off in his sleep, and he lay with the left side of his head upward. And Tom's eyes, accustomed to the dim starlight, could see that under the lank hair there was no ear, but only a hideous sear. The boy shivered as he lay down and from that time onward until dawn his thoughts circled feverishly about the sinister figure of the steersman.

When morning came, Tom wasted no time. Immediately after breakfast had been eaten he came to his uncle, in the cabin, and told him of Andy's presence in the boat. When he came to the riverboy's identification of Rogers as a member of the Wilson gang, Ezra Lockwood shook his head, incredulously. "The lad's imagination has run away with him," he said. " 'Earless Jake' he may be, and, too, the boy may have seen him in bad company. These rivermen are a wild lot—even the best of them. But to say that he's no pilot is foolish. He's done well by us so far, at least. Then, too, the fellow knows the Colemans—brought 'em down last year. What would your Andy say to that?"

"Rogers only *says* he knows the Colemans," Tom reminded his uncle. "We've no real proof of it. And you aren't going to put him ashore, then?"

"Not until we reach a town, at least," said the older man. "Surely we could not set a man down, afoot in the wilderness, merely on suspicion!"

Tom was forced to be content with this answer, though he could not escape a feeling of uneasiness. The day went by for the most part uneventfully. One incident broke in harshly on the serenity of their progress, however, and it left an increased sense of foreboding in Tom's mind.

It was early afternoon, and the boy was fishing over the side. They had passed Maysville, on the Kentucky shore, and were moving steadily down with the current. "General Wayne," the pilot's pet raccoon, which had been given quarters on a square board at the top of the stubby mast, amidships, descended from his perch with a rattle of his chain and started toward a bone, left on the deck by Cub. The dog was lying asleep not ten feet away and something woke him just as the marauding 'coon reached his property. He jumped to the attack like an angry whirlwind, and caught the "General" before he could regain his pole. The fight was fierce but short. Though the 'coon lived up to his name as a battler, he was no match for the savage terrier. By the time Tom got to the scene the melee was over. Cub had broken his adversary's back.

Behind him, the boy heard a wild scream, and turned his head in time to see Jake Rogers hurtling over the edge of the afterdeck toward him. The man's face was twisted horribly and he had a long knife in his hand. Tom rose from above the dead 'coon and braced himself to meet the onslaught. But no attack came. The pilot checked himself with an effort, and forced the lips over his clenched teeth into a twisted smile. Slowly he put the knife back into its sheath at his side.

"I'll—I'll—well, nev' mind," he said, hoarsely, and with this strange speech he clambered back to his oar barely in time to keep the boat from swinging sidewise. There was a hint of ferocity held in leash in the man's manner that gave Tom a creepy sensation.

Tom settled down by the rail and fished the rest of the afternoon. His line, at least, was in the water, but the hook was unbaited. In his mind the boy was busily turning over the events of the month that had passed since his party crossed the mountains. Many little happenings which had seemed odd at the time now came back to puzzle him. There was the evil-faced native in the canoe, for instance. If, as Tom had begun to suspect, the waving of the man's paddle had been some sort of signal to Rogers, it seemed quite probable that the two had plotted together before—in Pittsburgh, perhaps. He thought of Rogers' first appearance at the wagon camp, and his suave talk of the Colemans. Then in a flash he remembered the conversation around the supper table at the tavern in the Alleghenies.

Had Ezra Lockwood spoken of the Colemans? Tom thought that he had. And the native had sat there listening, but—yes, the surly innkeeper had given him a look of some sort—he recalled it all now. And in the night, the blanketed figure had vanished—not without some assistance from within, for the door had been barred again. Was it possible that the

German, who had seen his uncle's fat wallet, had sent the native with a message to confederates at the head of the Ohio? The longer he thought, the surer Tom became that there was a plot afoot to rob them.

At last he could stand it no longer. He hauled in his line and started to go aft. The sun was setting in the big trees on the Kentucky shore, and Tom saw that Rogers had already swung the nose of the *Phoebe Ann* in toward the left bank for the night landing.

The place where they moored was a small, deep cove, overhung by huge oaks. It was nearly dark under the trees, but a cheery campfire was soon blazing, and preparations for supper went forward apace. Tom stole back to the boat, once all were gathered around the fire, and pulled Andy from his hiding-place.

"While we are at supper, take the rifle here, and slip ashore," Tom whispered. "Wait for me up the bank a little way, and I'll bring you something to eat."

While the meal was in progress, Tom managed, unobserved, to slip some bread and meat into a leather pouch, and when the rest of the party climbed back aboard the boat, he took his own rifle and an ax and stole off in the direction of the spot he had indicated to Andy.

The riverboy was waiting for him. Ravenously he attacked the food Tom had brought, and as he ate, Tom told him what had happened that day.

"I heard the racket when that dog o' yourn killed the 'coon," Andy whispered. "Lordy, boy, you was close to a goner! Earless Jake would a stuck ye with that knife quicker'n chain lightnin', only he's got somethin' up his sleeve. I never seen him hold back thataway before."

"He's planning some kind of devilry—I'm sure of that, now," Tom answered. "And I can't convince Uncle Ezra. It's up to you and me, I guess, Andy. Come on up the bank a way and we'll make some plans of our own."

They stepped noiselessly along under the trees till they reached a place where they could talk without being heard. Cub came close behind, and when they seated themselves on a fallen tree trunk, he trotted about nearby.

The boys had not been in the place more than five minutes when the little dog suddenly jumped close to Tom's knee, and stood rigid, his head turned in the direction of the landing. The hair was rising along his spine, and a faint premonitory growl shivered in his throat.

Both lads rose, alert to catch whatever sound of warning had already reached the terrier's ears. The wind was from behind them, and blew downriver toward the boat. They could hear nothing but the sigh of the breeze in the pine branches.

Cub's hearing was keener, however. He started forward a few steps, his growl growing louder. Then with a bound he was off, down the shore, and almost at the same instant the boys heard a yell, half smothered by the wind.

"Come quick," said Tom, and started at a run in the direction of the boat. As they drew close to the landing, the sound of a shot reached them, followed by a man's hoarse scream of pain. There was a confused sound of scuffling, and then a great shout, in a voice that both boys recognized as that of Rogers, "We've got 'em all—shove off!"

Tom sprang down upon the bank with his rifle half raised. The keelboat's mooring had been cut, and now she floated clear of the shore, and was just beginning to catch the current.

"Stop or I'll shoot!" cried Tom, and at the same instant took aim at the dim shape of the man by the steering oar. There was no reply. The woods echoed to the report of the boy's rifle and the helmsman let go his sweep with a snarl of anguish. A spattering volley from half a dozen guns answered Tom's fire,

and a storm of oaths came over the water. Andy stood beside his friend, and he too brought his rifle to his shoulder, but Tom checked him, "Don't shoot wild," he said. "You might hit some of our own folks!"

A moment later the boat slid out of sight past the point that formed the lower side of the cove.

Tom's rifle butt dropped to the ground with a thud. He passed his hand aimlessly across his face. "Well," he said at length, in a dull voice, "we were too late, after all. Andy—tell me—what'll those devils do to my Aunt and Uncle?"

"Jiminy, Tom, I don't know!" choked the smaller boy. "Sometimes they hold 'em prisoner fer a long time. Sometimes they—well—never mind—we got to git out o' this now. They might land a couple o' men to come back an' pick us off. Le's go up river a ways."

They went back along the shore, heavy of heart. Cub, running by Tom's side, whimpered a little in sympathy, and tried to shove his cold nose into the boy's hand. At length Andy, who was in the lead, stumbled out of the underbrush into a little open space with a knoll in the middle.

"They won't come up's fur's this," he said. "'Sides, this moss is too nice an' soft to pass by. I didn't sleep a wink last night, nor all day today, neither. Come mornin' we kin tell better what to do."

This logic met with no objection from Tom, who was himself so weary he could hardly stand. They tumbled into the deep carpet of moss on the knoll, and lying close together for warmth, were instantly asleep.

CHAPTER IX

Tom struggled upward out of an abyss of sleep and lay, semiconscious, wondering what made his legs feel so stiff. Without opening his eyes he put out a hand and fumbled about beside him. Funny—the deck felt wet—had it rained, he wondered? The happy singing of the thrush that had first wakened him had a fair-weather sound. Was it daylight yet? They would be starting down the river soon—

In a flash he remembered where he was, and sat bolt upright, his eyes blinking in the morning sunlight. Beside him, in the little glade, Andy still slumbered, his mouth peacefully open, and a half-smile on his freckled face. Tom wouldn't wake him yet. He got to his feet and looked around him. The dew was heavy in the moss, and it was sleeping there without blankets that had stiffened him. A dry branch in the thicket crackled and Cub came trotting into the open space. The little dog seemed to care nothing at all for their predicament. He dashed to Tom's side with a cheerful greeting of tail wags and wet kisses. Tom rolled him over in the grass and started down to the riverbank, a score of yards away.

A douse in the cold water raised the lad's spirits wonderfully. The sun came up and with it a little breeze that ruffled the river pleasantly, and as he sprang up the bank once more, Tom was actually whistling.

From the ground near where he had slept he picked up the ax, thrown down in dejection the night before. The feel of the ash helve in his hand was good. Going into the brush, higher up the bank, Tom soon cut half a dozen dead birches into firewood lengths and carried several armfuls down to the knoll. Then he took his rifle, loaded it carefully, without spilling a grain of the precious powder that filled his big powder horn, and stepped off into the woods.

Cub, though not a bird dog, had been taught by many hunting trips with his owner that he must not bark. Now he trotted quietly ahead, and before they had proceeded a quarter of a mile he flushed a partridge. The bird flew a few yards and sat foolishly on a pine limb. Probably it had never seen a dog or a man before. Tom fired, deliberately, as usual, and the partridge dropped, scarcely fluttering. With the plump fowl swinging from his gun barrel, the boy went back to camp.

A cheery sight welcomed him at the edge of the cleared space. Dry sticks were snapping in a tidy little blaze and Andy, standing bareheaded nearby, was humming a river ditty as he shaped a crude bucket out of birchbark.

"Gee!" he cried, hungrily, as he caught sight of Tom's trophy, "Got a pa'tridge, did ye? I heard the ol' gun shoot. Come on— clean the little feller, an' I'll cook ye the best breakfast in Kaintuck!"

There was no flour for pancakes—no coffee nor tea—nothing but the fat little bird which soon sizzled above the fire, spitted on a green stick. Yet these two wilderness-raised lads found their meal a delicious and satisfying one. Andy had in a pocket of his coat one of the little leather sacks of salt that woodsmen of that day often carried, and with this they seasoned their breakfast. Tom had brought a gallon of muddy water up from the river in the birchbark dipper.

"We'll go to the spring, down by the landing, after this," he said, "but river water won't hurt us this morning."

They picked the bones of the partridge and sat down on the river bank to consider their case.

"Now, Andy," said Tom, "S'pose you were Earless Jake. What do you reckon you'd do with Uncle Ezra and Aunt Phoebe?"

Andy scowled, and drove his long hunting knife into the sod, speculatively. Finally he answered, "Wal, if I was that mean cuss, which I ain't, I figger I'd tie 'em both up in the hold o' the boat, an' put fer ol' Jericho Wilson's cave. Onct I got down thar, I wouldn't be 'fraid o' nothin'. I'd keep 'em prisoner a while, 'cause I'd cal'late that folks as well fixed as them would hev friends back east willin' to pay fer 'em.

"As fer you, Tom," Andy added with a grin, "I reckon if I was ol' Jake, I'd say to myself, 'Huh! That 'ar leetle varmint! He'll starve to death in a week!'" And the redhaired lad rolled agilely out of the way, as Tom's hand descended.

The bigger boy laughed. "At that," he said, "I believe you're right. Jake never did seem to make much account of me. He'll figure I'm as good as dead already." The thoughtful look gave place to a gleam in Tom's eyes, and he sat up straight in the sunlight. "All right, Andy," he said, "we're going to show that lowdown cur! He doesn't know that there's two of us, remember."

Tom stood up and squared his shoulders as he looked down the river. His mouth was set in a grim line. "How many days will it take 'em to reach Jericho Wilson's cave?" he asked.

"Let's see," Andy pondered, "one to the Licking River, an' Cincinnati, one, two—three more days to the Falls, then maybe a day waitin' to go down. After that, four days or maybe five to the Wabash. Jericho's hangout is close below—only three or four hours, say. Ye can call it ten days, ordinary goin'. If they was to travel nights they could cut that down to less'n a week, but I don't see why they should be in much of a hurry."

"Good," said Tom. "We'll say nine days, to be on the safe

side. Now, Andy, I mean to catch that boat before it reaches the Wabash. There'd probably be another keelboat or broadhorn along here within a couple of days if we wanted to wait, though I don't think this is a regular landing place. But they wouldn't make any better time than Jake and his crew. We've got to go in our own craft, and go night and day, if we hope to overtake the *Phoebe Ann*.

"Andy, did you ever build a canoe?"

"Nope," said the riverboy. "But I've seen 'em built, birchbarks an' dugouts both, an' oh, boy, I sure can paddle one!"

"Same here," Tom nodded. "I've been looking around and there don't seem to be any big birch trees along this part of the river—nothing but these little gray birches. And then, even if we found a good canoe tree, it takes time to get the pitch and the lacings in shape to use. No, Andy, it's got to be a dugout, and we've got to get to work on it in an all-fired hurry!"

"Come on," said Andy, "I seen a big gum tree up the shore this mornin'," and jumping to his feet he started off at a trot. The tree to which he led the way was over three feet in diameter and tall and straight of trunk. The new leaves coming out on all its branches bore witness to its soundness. "She'll be heavy and full of sap," said Tom, "but it's the best we can do, this time of year." And even as he spoke, his free-swung ax bit deep into the wood.

For nearly two hours the light chips flew and the sharp ring of steel on wood sounded through the forest, as first one boy and then the other took his turn at the deepening "scarf."

At length Andy, looking aloft, gave a warning shout, "Here she comes!" and Tom, with a final mighty stroke of the ax, sprang nimbly to one side. The huge tree tottered slowly, swaying toward the river, then gathered momentum and came down with a roar of rending fibers and a jarring crash as it struck the earth.

"Don't look much like a boat, does she?" grinned Andy.

"Here, Tom, lend me the ax, an' while you figger how long to make her, I'll go cut us a couple o' wedges an' a spud."

Tom sighted carefully along the fallen trunk, noticed that there was a knot about twenty feet from the base, and decided that the place to cut was just below this protuberance. Andy soon returned with several roughly shaped wedges of white oak, which he proceeded to finish with his hunting knife, and Tom, taking the ax once more, fell to work chopping the great trunk in two.

They labored without pause till it was long past noon. Then Tom straightened up and looked at his calloused hands.

"That'll do," he said. "There's less than a foot left in the middle. We can burn that through while we're getting some dinner."

He threw a few handfuls of dry chips and twigs in a heap under the nearly severed tree, and put one hand into his pocket for flint and steel. A delighted grin overspread his face. "Gee, what luck!" he cried. "I was just wondering what we'd have to eat. Look here, Andy—the fish line I was using yesterday—I stuck it in my pocket when we landed. Boy, I'll have a catfish out of water in three minutes!"

He was almost as good as his word, for an hour later the boys had dined, rested, and were ready for work once more. As Tom had prophesied, the brisk little fire had burned away the remaining wood between the tree trunk and what the boys already called their canoe.

Now came the long, difficult process of splitting the green wood. Tom had helped his uncle get out timber from the time he could swing an ax, and Andy was no less an adept, although he did not possess Tom's strength. Gradually, inch by inch, they drove their oak wedges deeper into the widening cleft that ran along the log, till at last the two halves separated cleanly and fell apart.

Andy grinned as he wiped the sweat from his forehead with one ragged sleeve. "Pretty stuff, ain't it?" he said, looking at the straight, fine grain of the wood.

The rift had been purposely made three or four inches to one side of the log's center, so that one part was slightly thicker than the other. It was to this larger piece that the boys now directed their attention. Not without some difficulty they turned it over with the bark upward, and fell to work shaping the bow and stern. Tom sharpened the ax on a flat stone and attacked one end, while Andy started a new fire at the other. By the time it grew too dark to work there was a crude semblance of an overturned boat lying on the river bank. Somewhat to the surprise of both, Andy's end was more nearly finished than Tom's.

"We can use the fire on the inside and get it burned out faster than we could chop it with the ax," said Tom. "Besides, the heat'll help to dry her out and make her lighter in the water." He stretched his arms above his head. "Ho, hum!" he yawned. "I sure am tired tonight. Hello there, Cub, old boy, what's up now?"

The little dog had been gone the best part of the afternoon. Now he came racing through the trees and rushed up to Tom, barking excitedly. Hardly had he reached his owner's side when he bounded away to the edge of the open space once more, looking back at the boys with eager eyes. Plainly he was begging them to come with him.

"Look at that!" said Tom, dropping his voice to a whisper. "Cub's found something, sure. It can't be any of Rogers' gang though or he wouldn't act this way. Here, boy, come back. It's too dark to go now, but I'll follow you in the morning."

And carefully priming their long rifles, the two lads turned in on a bed of fresh-cut pine tips.

CHAPTER X

T HE FIRST SLANT beam of morning sun found the glade by the riverbank abustle with activity. The boys had made such a breakfast as they could off the perch that rose to Andy's hook. The diet of fish alone was already beginning to pall, however.

"Tom," said the redhaired riverboy, as he fed the fire, "soon as we git the boat turned over again, I'll start burnin' her out an' you go after some meat. Gosh, I'll grow a pair o' gills if I eat fish again today!"

They rolled the half log back, with its split side upward, and Tom shouldered his rifle. Cub jumped up with a joyous bound as he saw what his owner was doing.

"All right, little dog," said the tall youngster, "now if you're still anxious to show me, I'll go see what you've found."

There was no question of Cub's eagerness. He was off like a shot through the trees, and Tom swung after him at his long woodsman's stride. The dog took a course up the hillside, then over the ridge, and led the way straight as an arrow into the big dark woods beyond. For nearly an hour he held this direction. Tom had gone part of the way at a trot, and he judged the distance they had covered to be at least five miles, when Cub stopped and looked up at his owner.

"What's the matter, boy—lost the trail?" asked Tom. The dog trotted on a few paces and sat down, his head cocked upward knowingly. A strange, low sound, of which Tom's ears had been vaguely aware for some time, now fully entered his consciousness. It seemed to come from the air all about him— a sort of faint, broken murmur. "Wild bees!" he thought, but he knew at once that this was not the sound of bees. He looked upward through the tender green of the young leaves, and saw, in the treetops, a number of dark, irregular masses, each a foot or so across.

"Nests!" he whispered to himself. Cub had led him to the nesting place of the wild pigeons!

The boy took a few eager strides forward into the woods and the sound in the trees above deepened into a throaty, vibrant hum—the cooing of thousands upon thousands of pairs of mating birds.[1]

There were pigeons everywhere in the branches and on the ground, some building nests, others foraging for food among the beech buds and the last year's mast that still lay here and there underfoot.

Tom could almost have knocked the birds over with a stick. He killed a score or more with only five shots, and slung them in a great bunch from his gun barrel. Then he moved forward through the nesting place, filling his eyes with the strange sight. In many of the trees every branch big enough to bear any weight held from one to a dozen nests, and this condition was not confined to a mere acre or two. The crowded breeding grounds seemed to stretch away for miles to the south and west. There must have been millions of the pretty, long-tailed, gray birds within the sound of a gunshot.

The sun was high, now, and Tom turned regretfully to retrace his steps. He had come nearly to the top of the long ridge that overlooked the valley of the Ohio, when Cub, trotting through the underbrush a hundred yards upwind, suddenly burst into a frenzy of barking. Tom dropped the pigeons hastily and held his rifle ready. It was fortunate that he did so, for at that instant a young buck came bounding down through the trees, sailed gracefully over a tangle of brush and paused, startled, not twenty yards from where Tom

---

1. Passenger pigeons, extinct since 1914.

stood. The rifle was at his shoulder and he fired before the deer could spring away. At that distance the bullet plowed through the buck's heart and dropped him where he stood.

This was luck, indeed. By his morning's work Tom had bagged enough food to last a week or more. He swung the hundred and twenty pound deer to his shoulder with a mighty heave, and staggered on over the ridge toward camp.

The pleasant smell of wood smoke greeted him. Andy had made some progress in burning out the canoe, and he gave a whoop of delight when he saw Tom's burden.

"We'll have the boat all ready in three more days," he cried, "an' you've got 'nough meat there to take us clean to the Wabash. 'Sides, ye kin work a sight harder on deer's meat 'n' pigeons 'n ye kin on catfish!"

Tom set about skinning and dressing the buck, while Andy broiled a pair of pigeons over the hot coals of his fire.

"Found a salt lick, this mornin'," called the riverboy, "right above here, close to the riverbank. They was deer tracks around there, too, only I didn't have time to wait fer 'em to come."

"Say, Andy," Tom answered, "why couldn't we salt some of the pigeons? They'd keep fine that way."

"We kin," said the redhaired lad, enthusiastically. "I been usin' the salt already, to keep the sides o' the canoe from burnin'. The fire comes to the edge o' the salt an' stops, jes' as clean as a whistle."

When they had finished their meal, both boys set to work once more on their dugout. Removing the inside of the log was a slow process at best. The fire did not burn away much wood at a time, and it left uneven places that had to be trimmed with the ax. For two days more they labored almost incessantly on the canoe. Tom spent the third morning in shaping long-bladed, stout paddles of white maple, while Andy was putting the finishing touches to the boat. The fire had dried out the sap so that the hull was surprisingly light, for all its thickness of three or four inches. By using sapling trunks for rollers, the boys had no difficulty in getting their craft down to the river and launching it. To their relief it rode high and evenly in the water.

The pigeons had been cleaned and stuffed with salt, and these, together with the venison, the ax and a spare paddle, they packed into the middle of the canoe. A place for Cub to lie was prepared amid this baggage. By sunset all preparations for departure had been made. The boys climbed in and took their places at bow and stern, and five days, to the hour, after the *Phoebe Ann* had first landed on that shore, the *Defiance*—frigate of two guns—so christened by Tom, stole out into the muddy current and shot away downstream into the gathering dark.

Andy, who was many pounds lighter than Tom, had the bow paddle.

"Goes fast, don't she?" he whispered over his shoulder, as he dipped the sharp blade. "I know the river pretty fair, below here. There ain't no snags nor bars to speak of 'twixt here'n the Bear Grass, if we stay in the channel. Jumpin' Jonah, look at that bank go past!"

Indeed the buoyant little dugout seemed to move more rapidly than the sluggish freight carriers, even without the aid of the paddles. Possibly the fact that the boys were so much closer to the water strengthened this impression. But certain it was that when they were both paddling, the little craft made nearly double the speed of any unwieldy keelboat or broadhorn.

They pushed on steadily for four hours. Sometimes one would rest while the other paddled; sometimes both would hold the long, even stroke for mile after mile. It must have been nearly eleven o'clock when Tom steered in for the Kentucky shore. A setting half-moon threw a pale light over the trees and enabled them to make a landing. They were far too weary to bother with a fire, but spread the deerskin on the ground and went to sleep, leaving Cub to stand guard.

A thrust of the dog's cold nose into his neck woke Tom at sunrise. He built a fire and washed, then called Andy and started broiling a piece of venison. Before the morning mist had wholly left the river they were back in the canoe and speeding downstream with the flood of brown waters. Soon they approached a great bend, where the river swung to the westward, and Andy said they would soon be passing the Cincinnati settlement.

"I knowed we wasn't fur above the Licking, last night," he said. "We'd best keep over to the Kaintuck side, 'cause they's sometimes a few o' Jericho's men hangin' 'round the wharf at Cincinnati."

The canoe rounded the bend and, running along almost in the shadow of the trees on the southern shore, cut across the mouth of the Licking River and passed over the sandy shallows on the lower side. As they swung out into the channel once more, Tom cast a curious glance over his shoulder at the village nestling in the haze at the foot of the bluffs across the Ohio. This little town with the strange Roman name was already becoming a factor in the trade of the river. He half wished they might have landed there, outlaws or no outlaws, if there had not been such need for haste.

Heavy clouds overcast the sky as the morning advanced, and soon it was raining—a steady drizzle that seemed to find its way through deerhide and homespun alike and wet the boys to the skin. Hard work with the paddles kept them warm, however, and at noon they made a fire and ate their dinner in a snug, dry place under a jackpine.

After a short rest they embarked once more, and drove along down the river all through the rainy afternoon. It began to grow dark early, Andy figured that they had made nearly eighty miles since morning. They must be coming close to the mouth of the Kentucky River now, he said. As they watched the south bank for a sign of the mouth of the stream, a flickering glow of light appeared among the trees. The canoe came swiftly down and Tom steered closer to the shore. The light shone brighter through the gusty darkness as they approached. Soon they saw that it came from a great bonfire on the bank. Below it two large boats were moored, and the figures of many men in buckskin stood or sat about the blaze. Rough voices, raised in song, rang across the water.

"I wouldn't git too close in, Tom, it don't look quite good to me," Andy was saying, when all of a sudden the boy at the stern paddle gave a whoop and, backing water sharply on the left, swung the bow of the dugout shoreward.

"That's Buckeye Ben Chandler and his Muskingum men!" Tom exclaimed. "I saw Hanson's bearskin cap when he crossed in front of the fire."

They made a landing just below the keelboats, and clambered up the bank into the circle of firelight. B'ar Hanson recognized Tom and bellowed a greeting. "Wal, I'll be a yaller-bellied puff-snake if 'tain't the young long hunter hisself!" he cried. "How come you ain't farther down the river, boy?"

Tom introduced Andy and told the story of their adventures while the grateful heat of the flames dried the boys' drenched clothing. When he came to the ambush and capture of the *Phoebe Ann* there was a nodding of heads among the hunters.

"We hed a visit from that same crew, the night arter you left Marietta," said Buckeye Ben, grimly. "One of 'em snuck aboard my boat when I was ashore an' stole a lot o' flour an' bacon. Yep, we aim to pay a call on this Jericho feller, soon's we git down his way."

He rose and spat fiercely into the fire.

"You boys better go down 'long of us," said B'ar Hanson to Tom. "We're sure a-goin' to make Wilson think he tromped on a bumblebees' nest. Ye know," he lowered his voice, " 'twa'n't jest the flour an' bacon they got. They took Ol' Sal,' too, an' Buckeye'd ruther been sculped 'n to lose that 'ar rifle o' his."

Tom nodded. "I know," he said, "but before you can get there, something might happen to my folks. I reckon Andy and I'll keep a-going. It's too dark to see our way tonight, but on a clear night we'll be able to paddle four or five hours, an' that way we can make better than a hundred miles a day. We figure to catch 'em before they reach the Wabash."

Hanson whistled. "Five days' start!" he said. "Think you kin make that up?"

"We aim to," answered Tom. And after accepting a present of some flour and a frying pan, he and Andy bade the Muskingum men goodnight.

They found a place on the shore where the ground was fairly dry, spread their deerskin, and turned the canoe over to form a narrow shelter, propped up at one end by a root. The rain drummed on the wooden shell above them and lulled them to sleep.

CHAPTER XI

IN THE night the weather cleared.

While Buckeye Ben and his hunters were still soundly slumbering, under the keelboats' decks, Tom and Andy rose, swallowed some cooked venison leftover from the day before, and launched their dugout. In the gray light of dawn they stole past the high cliffs that marked the mouth of the Kentucky, and by the time the sun came up and birds began to sing in the trees they were already half a dozen miles downstream.

As on the previous day they paddled and rested by turns, logging off a fairly steady ten miles an hour. The vast curves of the river unwound before them, swirling past steep bluffs and long, easy slopes where the trees of the age-old wilderness grew tall and dense like a forest of glistening green towers.

Before noon they had made half a hundred miles. And now Andy, crouching in the bow, swung around to grin at Tom. "Feel her startin' to speed up?" he asked. "We'd better begin huggin' the Kaintuck bank a leetle closer. Ol' rips sure do pull ye in, if ye don't take keer. Listen—no, not yet, I guess—but we'll hear 'em talkin' in a minute."

Tom edged the craft over till she was running hardly a hundred yards from shore. Soon, as Andy had promised, there became audible a faint rumbling sound, at first hardly more than a vibration in the air. The canoe was shooting forward at a much more rapid rate than before, and the surface of the river was pocked and pitted with rippling eddies. Below, at the left, a town came into view, and a creek mouth above it, with many flatboats moored.

"Swing in, an' paddle hard!" cried Andy. "Thar's Louisville an' the Bear Grass!"

For the next minute or two neither boy had time to look about much. Both were driving in their blades like mad, in an effort to reach the slack water at the mouth of the creek. But the current, running like a mill race, carried them down faster and faster.

"No use!" yelled Andy. "We've got to take it! Sit tight an' steer as I tell ye."

The boys had talked often of the descent of the Falls in the week they had been together. Andy had told Tom that it was possible for a canoe, manned by skilled rivermen, to live through the two-mile stretch of whitewater, though few pilots cared to try it in any craft smaller than a flatboat.

He had said, Tom now remembered, that the safer channel ran to the right of the rocky island that split the current halfway down the rips. Without more ado he wrenched the bow around to the right with a mighty twist of his paddle, and began digging in fiercely on the left side of the canoe.

The dugout, spinning downward at terrific speed, now edged out farther into midstream in response to these efforts. Ahead, and coming swiftly closer, Tom could see the jagged black snout of the rock. He threw every atom of his strength into his paddle strokes. Andy, too, was working for his life, and inch by inch the canoe was being driven sidewise, across the rushing current.

A gasping cry came from Andy but the roar of the rapids drowned his words. The black rock was only seconds away, now. Tom thrust desperately, with weary arms, again and yet again, and they went past by the breadth of a hand and shot down the flume of white water that swept along the island's northern side.

The boys crouched, waiting, in the bottom of the dugout and steadied themselves for the next struggle. It was on them almost at once. The level lane of water down which they were driving broke suddenly into leaping waves and their craft began dancing like an eggshell.

Andy had spoken truth when he said that he was at home in a canoe. Coolly now he balanced at the forward end of the narrow hull, and with quick, sure motions, plunged his paddle on one side or the other. Occasionally he would flash a hand out as a signal to Tom, who instantly steered in the direction he pointed. So they flew down, zigzagging among the cruel teeth of the rocks, tossing through white torrents of spray, and shipping water sometimes by the bucketful—yet right side up still. And then Andy, unable to make himself heard above the thunder of the Falls, held up both hands in a gesture that could only mean, "Steady as she is—stop paddling," and Tom waited breathless. There was a long second in which the canoe seemed to hang motionless on the rushing water. Then she leaped out into the mist, dropped and struck with a jarring tremor, rocked perilously once—twice—steadied, and flew on unscathed. They were over the four-foot "shelf" at last.

A moment more and the boys had left the whitewater behind. Their canoe still glided on rapidly, but the roar of the tumbling waters was dying behind them. Tom steered in toward the Kentucky shore, and five minutes later they were building a fire on the firm brown sod, where the mutter of the rapids came only faintly to their ears.

While the venison sputtered with a delicious smell, Tom stretched out on his back and looked into the sky. "Never knew how good the hard ground could feel, before," he chuckled.

Cub, wet with spray and abjectly shivering, cuddled close to his owner's side.

"Pore leetle feller!" laughed Andy. "Reckon he didn't think he'd ever git ashore ag'in. Wal, I warn't so 'tarnal sure of it myself, once or twice."

The boy's face grew sober as he looked back at the racing water below the Falls. "You know," he said, half hesitantly, "'twas in them rips I lost my Pappy. He was a fine big feller, an' a fust class pilot, too, if he hadn't took a leetle too much corn licker now an' then. He warn't allus a riverman, ye see, an' 'twas thinkin' about the ol' times when he was rich, an' 'mounted to somethin', that useter start him on one o' his sprees. 'Course, me bein' sech a youngster, he never tolt me much, but one time, when his tongue was loosened up with a jug, he did talk to me. I couldn't understand much of it then—I was too leetle—but thinkin' it over an' puttin' bits together, since, I've got an idee the story runs sort o' like this:

"My Pappy come from Virginny, when I warn't much more'n a baby. Back there he owned a great big plantation with slaves an' hosses by the hundreds, I reckon. But somehow there was a fight about his wife—my mother—that I never could understand. An' after that he sold all his land, and houses, an' got a heap o' money together, an' come over the Blue Ridge, totin' me along. He was headin' fer the Spanish colonies on the Mississippi, an' he aimed to buy up 'bout half o' Louisiana, I guess, an' start off fresh.

"Wal, when he got to the Bear Grass, he found a lot o' men racin' hosses in the street o' Louisville, an' he had a mare that could run. So he went in with his mare an' won the race an' a lot o' bets with it. But that night, when he was buyin' drinks fer the town, at the tavern, somebody went to the boats, where they was three or four men guardin' the money, an' killed 'em all, an' stole the boats, an' the mare, an' all my father owned, ceptin' me an' the clothes we stood up in.

"He tried his best to find out who done it an' git the law on 'em, but there warn't no law on the river those days, no more'n there is now. He'd cut loose fer good from all his friends in Virginny. Only thing he could do was stay in Louisville an' wait fer somethin' to turn up. He got to takin' boats through the rips, fer he warn't afeared o' nothin'. An' then he started in drinkin' harder an'—wal—that's about all."

They ate their broiled venison in silence. Tom was the first to speak, after it was finished. "How long has this man Wilson been on the river?" he asked, irrelevantly.

"Jericho?" said Andy, returning from his thoughts, "Oh, he's one o' the ol' timers. Some says he come up the river from N'Orleans, with soldiers arter him fer some devilry or other. There's another yarn about him bein' taken prisoner when he was a boy an' brought up with the Choctaw around some French fort. Anyhow, he's been 'round these parts ten years—fifteen, maybe. I set eyes on him jest once, down at the cave a couple o' years ago, an' I'll never forget him. Biggest man I ever see—big around as a hogshead, I'll bet!"

Andy had picked up the empty frying pan as he talked, and now started toward the river to wash it. But as be reached the bank he saw a sight that made him call back to Tom, excitedly. Less than half a mile away, and coming down at racehorse speed through the last of the white water, was a big flatboat. Tom had run to Andy's side at his hail, and together they watched the square-nosed craft shoot forward to the lip of the shelf, lunge out with half her length clear of the water, and strike the lower level with a splash that sent the spray high on either side. A single dark figure balanced erect near the stern and swung the long handle of the tiller deftly from side to side, as the broadhorn came careering past.

Andy's eyes were glowing. "Thar!" he said. "That's the kind o' thing my Dad used to do!"

The flatboat cut in for the shore just below the boys' landing place, and a moment later, as they were loading their canoe preparatory to making a fresh start, the pilot came up the bank, afoot. He was a tall, rangy, sandy-haired Kentuckian.

"You boys come through the rips in that canoe?" he asked, as he drew abreast. "Good steerin'—good steerin'. Now, only three days ago I seen a keelboat come a-r'arin' down thar—a big new one she was, too—"

"Wait," cried Tom, "was her name in green on the bows—*Phoebe Ann?*"

"Same boat," nodded the pilot. "She jes' got through by the skin of her teeth, an' no more—"

But Tom and Andy had already thrown their duffel into the dugout and were launching it. "Three days ahead of us, you say," Tom cried. "Then we've got to start and start quick!"

Cub tumbled in, barking excitedly, and they were off once more.

CHAPTER XII

THE RIVER, after its thirty-foot drop at the Falls, still ran swiftly for many miles, and its channel was beset by bars and rocky shoals. Rough hills, cut by ravines and thickly wooded, went up on either hand—as wild and beautiful a country as the boys had ever seen.

It was approaching dusk when they rounded a bend some thirty-five miles below Louisville, and saw far ahead a small, dilapidated looking flatboat making her sluggish way downstream. There were rocks to the left of the channel, and the only course for the canoe lay alongside the ancient broadhorn. The boys came swiftly down till they were close astern, when Andy stopped paddling suddenly and looked back at Tom with a frightened face.

"Gee!" he whispered, "that's one o' Jericho Wilson's boats. I'd know her anywheres—used to be aboard of her."

"Well," Tom replied, "there's nothing for it now but to go past. Come on!"

They were almost under the flatboat's counter. Andy seized his paddle and together the boys drove their blades vigorously. Just then a startled voice sounded from close above on the deck of the broadhorn, and there was a rush of feet to the side. Tom and Andy crouched low and paddled desperately, without looking up. Their canoe shot past the bow of the larger craft and on into open water, below.

"Hold on, thar!" shouted a deep, angry voice—a voice they both had heard before—and a second later came the cracking report of a rifle. A bullet sang dangerously close.

"Lie down!" yelled Tom, and both boys tumbled flat in the bottom of the dugout.

Hardly had Tom and Andy flung themselves face downward in the canoe when a scattered volley from half a dozen rifles struck the little craft. At least one of the bullets plowed through the bottom and others splintered the thick gunwales. A spent slug grazed Andy's leg and drew an ugly looking stream of blood.

Meanwhile the canoe's momentum had slackened and she no longer drew away from the flatboat but remained within easy gunshot. Something had to be done. Tom, thinking fast, decided that most of the guns on the broadhorn must have been discharged, and that he would run less risk of being shot now, than a moment later, when some of the outlaws had had a chance to reload. He gripped his paddle and rose quickly to his knees once more. Frantically he thrust the blade over the side and drove the canoe forward with half a dozen swift strokes. A single rifle was fired behind him and the bullet swept the coonskin cap from his head. He ducked instinctively, then straightened again and paddled desperately on. Surely they must have their guns ready by now. He waited, with a chilly feeling down his spine, for the next shot, but still he kept on at feverish speed. Andy, too, was paddling now. Why didn't they shoot? At last Tom cast a hurried look over his shoulder, and to his amazement saw that the flatboat was out of gunshot, hundreds of yards in the rear.

The boy dropped back, gasping, and wiped the cold sweat from his forehead. Andy turned and grinned back at him but he was pale under his freckles.

"Great wallopin' rattlesnakes!" he panted. "That's a measly feelin', ain't it—somebody a-poppin' at the back o' yer neck when you can't git under cover! Say, Tom, here's a leetle hole in the bottom that's lettin' the river in right smart."

"How big is it?" asked Tom.

" 'Bout the size o' my finger, an' round," Andy replied. "Here, I'll stuff a piece o' my shirt in it, jest fer now. Lucky we brung along that old birchbark bucket. I'll bail her out while you paddle."

They ran on down the river for two hours till the night had fallen black, then landed on a little island in midstream. Here they figured they were far enough ahead of the river pirates to build a fire, and soon they were ravenously attacking their evening meal. That finished, Tom whittled a peg to fit the bullet hole in the canoe, which, firmly driven in, rendered the craft as tight as ever. Andy's wound, meanwhile, had been dressed as carefully as possible, with the crude means they had at their disposal. Fortunately the bullet had not cut an artery and the bleeding was easily staunched.

"I got a sneakin' feelin' I know the feller that fired that shot," the river lad said. "That voice sounded like Black Carnahan to me."

"Me, too," answered Tom briefly. "Let's get going."

Without longer delay the boys doused their fire and embarked once more.

"If we can get down maybe twenty miles farther before we sleep," said Tom, "I figure we'll be only about a hundred miles back of Earless Jake and the *Phoebe Ann*. It'll take them two more days to reach the cave, and us not quite so long. We'll catch 'em yet, Andy."

They camped that night on the north bank, in the Indiana country. There was a stream running into the Ohio just below them which Andy thought was called "Blue River" by the pilots. Next morning they were awake and ready to start before daybreak. Andy's leg had stiffened somewhat in the night, but otherwise appeared to be doing well, and he found no difficulty in sitting in the canoe. Tom did most of the paddling.

They saw no settlements that day, but only league upon league of wild, unbroken forests. They were coming into the country of the lower river, a region teeming with newly awakened forest life in the spring weather, and as untouched by human hands as on the day when the first French voyageur drifted down with the current. An occasional desolate cabin, built by some hunter strayed from Kentucky, was the only habitation they passed.

By the time darkness fell they had covered another hundred miles, and Tom, utterly weary, was willing to turn in without attempting any night paddling. They slept on a bushy island near the mouth of Little Pigeon Creek.

When the Pennsylvania boy woke he found the sun already shining and Andy grimly at work, cleaning the guns and sharpening his knife.

"We'll reach the Wabash sure today," he exclaimed. "Mebbe we'll git to use these things afore night."

All that morning they went down past the long islands that now divided the river. One village of perhaps twenty houses on the Kentucky shore—a place called Henderson—was the only settlement they sighted. At noon a great wooded island, appeared ahead of them. They steered into the northern channel, and for nearly half an hour as they shot downstream the high banks of the island continued on their left hand. When at length the open river came into view, below, Andy said that they would be at the Wabash in three more hours.

Tom was far too eager to overtake the keelboat to stop for a midday meal. They drove along through the afternoon without a pause, and at last, when the sun was dropping low in the west, Andy pointed silently ahead. There below them, Tom saw the broad mouth of a big river entering the Ohio.

They paddled across the swirling eddies where the currents ran together, and came into the head of the long straight stretch beyond. As the view opened out for leagues ahead, Andy gave a sudden exclamation and rose to his knees, shading his eyes with one hand.

"What sort o' boat would ye call that, Tom?" he asked.

The Pennsylvania boy swung the canoe so that he too had an uninterrupted view of the river. There, perhaps two miles downstream, was a good-sized craft, unpainted but built of lumber bright and new.

"That's a keelboat," answered Tom, after a moment's scrutiny, "and unless I'm away off it's the *Phoebe Ann!*"

"Jes' what I thought," Andy said, "Now, what's your plan?"

"Well," Tom pondered, "I've been waiting to see how the land lays. Of course, what I aim to do first is find out if my Uncle Ezra and Aunt Phoebe are still aboard. We'll have to keep behind till it's dark and then sneak up and do some scouting. I'm not so sure, now, that they aren't watching for us. Seems as if they must have told the crew of that old barge we passed up above that we might be along soon. They wouldn't have been so quick to shoot if they hadn't known who we were."

"I dunno 'bout that," Andy answered. "When they're lickered up, them boys o' Jericho's shoot first an' talk arterwards. Still, it's possible they was watchin' fer you.

"Now let's see. At the rate they're a-goin' they couldn't reach the cave in less'n four hours more. An' the landin' there ain't one you'd want to make in the dark. They'll likely tie up to the bank an' go on down in the mornin'. That'll be our chance, while they're moored to shore."

The boys paddled on till they were less than a mile above the slow-moving keelboat, then drifted down, close to the northern shore, keeping a watchful eye on the craft ahead.

Andy's expectations were soon fulfilled. A little after sunset they saw the boat swing in toward the right bank and glide out of sight under the overhanging trees. When they were sure that the big craft had been made fast for the night, they themselves landed and cooked some meat over a little fire. Tom was too excited to eat more than a few mouthfuls—a fact which he was later to regret most bitterly.

The boys waited until night had fully fallen, then launched the dugout once more and paddled silently down to a wooded point, only a quarter of a mile above the keelboat.

"Now," said Tom, as they disembarked, "you and Cub stay here with the canoe, Andy. There's nothing to be gained by our both going on, and if it came to running away your leg would bother you. I'll be back here in an hour. If I don't come, you'll know they've got me."

Andy agreed to this plan, not without some grumbling, and Tom, carrying his long, keen skinning knife as his only weapon, set out down the shore.

A full moon was just rising, but the sky in the east was hazy and the light remained dim and uncertain. The tall young woodsman picked his way through the undergrowth, going slowly to avoid making any noise, and after what seemed a long time came out into a small uneven space beneath the trees.

The last graying embers of the outlaws' supper fire smoked in the middle of this opening. Close at hand against the bank lay the dark bulk of the *Phoebe Ann.* There was no sound or sign of life, either aboard the craft or on shore. Tom advanced stealthily till he stood within two paces of the keelboat's bow, and strained his eyes downward in an effort to see what lay in the dark on her forward planking. As he had expected, the open part of the boat was filled with the dim shapes of sleeping men. Softly, then, he stole back along the bank toward the decked-in after house, and placed one moccasin-clad foot on the poling plank that ran along the side. The big boat gave slightly under his weight, settling over with a soft creak of timbers. He waited, breathless, his heart pounding fiercely in his throat. No one onboard had been awakened. He prepared to shift his weight to the deck of the boat.

Then, as he crouched, a half-audible sound reached the boy's ears. It came from behind him. Even as he turned his head he saw the dark form of a man rising from the bank, a yard away. Caught off balance as he was, Tom instinctively flung up his left arm to guard himself, and it was none too soon. There came the quick, ugly *swish* of a descending tomahawk, and though the blow was half-broken by his arm, the edge of the ax cleft Tom's fur cap and fell with numbing force upon his skull.

He toppled backward to the deck, groping for his hunting knife, but before he could draw the blade from its sheath his antagonist had sprung upon him with a deep-throated yell— the first war-whoop that Tom had ever heard. The cry was answered by other voices, and while Tom wrestled desperately with his adversary, a dozen men clambered up from amidships.

The struggle was soon over. Still weak and dizzy from the blow on his head, Tom could put up no effectual resistance to the attack of the river pirates. He felt himself bound with a heavy cord of hemp and carried down to the after cabin where he was flung on the planking between two bales of goods. A moment later he lost consciousness.

CHAPTER XIII

When next Tom opened his eyes it was to a filter of daylight, coming through the square stern port of the keelboat's cabin. His head seemed to be on a pillow and a light hand stroked his cheek. His aunt sat beside him, and when she saw that he was awake she spoke, in her gentle Quaker manner.

"Does thy head hurt, Tom?" she asked.

He turned his face and smiled at her. "Not so very much. Aunt Phoebe," said he. "Where's Uncle Ezra—and Brad, and Danny?"

"Thy uncle is here, still asleep," she answered, dropping her voice to a whisper. "Brad is tied up, somewhere forward. Danny—poor Danny—they killed him, that night. They have treated us well enough so far, and we hope for the best. Oh, but it is good to have thee back once more—even here! I have prayed for thee, Tommy, many times. But rest, now, if thee can. They seem to be starting again."

Tom heard the rattle of a mooring rope thrown on deck and then the slow creak of the steering oar as the craft drifted out into the current. Then he lay still for what seemed hours, revolving in his mind the events that had led up to his capture. What, he wondered, would Andy do, now? He had no doubt that the lad would make every effort to save his friends, but it was difficult to see what he could accomplish, single-handed, against a robber gang that was reputed to number nearly a hundred men.

These reflections only seemed to increase the dull throb in his head, and after a time he grew restless. His hands and feet, he found, were tied behind in such a way that he could not sit up. While he was trying to work into a more comfortable position, three men came stooping into the cabin and stood over him. One was a stranger, roughly dressed, with an evil face, and another was a native. It was the same man who had tomahawked him the night before, and as he came closer, Tom realized with a start that this was the identical man he had seen twice earlier in his journey. The third man was Jake Rogers.

The lean pirate limped a step nearer and leered down at Tom with a sardonic grin. "Thought ye'd come back an' visit with the folks, did ye?" he chuckled. "Ain't quite big enough to take keer o' yerself yit, be ye? Wal, don't fret, boy—we'll take keer o' ye!" And the leather-faced outlaw gave his two companions a look which caused the first man to laugh uproariously and even brought a grin to the second man's face. As Earless Jake turned to go out, Tom saw that his right arm was wrapped in a clumsy bandage, and he took such satisfaction as he could from the thought that the treacherous pilot had not gone scatheless on the night the boat was captured.

Soon after the three rivermen had left, Ezra Lockwood awoke and greeted Tom. The boy would hardly have known his robust uncle in the gaunt, hollow-eyed man who sat before him, shackled to the sternpost. The last ten days had left their mark on him. Yet there was something of the old grim courage in his voice as he spoke to Tom.

"Surely, sooner or later, a time will come," he whispered, "when they will not guard us quite so closely. We must be ready to take our chance then—and die fighting if need be."

Tom nodded. He was beginning to feel more like himself now. The headache was gone, but he seemed to be terribly empty.

"Don't they give us any breakfast?" he asked.

"Usually they eat before starting," replied his uncle. "But this morning they cooked nothing. Perhaps they will wait till they reach the cave. I understand that will be soon."

Hardly had he finished speaking when they heard a loud hail from shore, answered by Rogers' voice on deck. The steering oar bore hard over and the boat veered to starboard. Soon there was a sound of running feet on the boards above, and the creak of a snubbing rope. The boat's side rubbed against timbers.

A jocular river pirate thrust his head into the cabin. "All ashore that's goin' to sleep at Wilson's tavern!" he shouted. Then began a great racket of unloading and in the midst of it Rogers entered. He had a crowbar in his hand, which he used to pry the massive staple of Ezra Lockwood's chain from the sternpost. Holding on to the end of the chain he approached Tom. "Guess there ain't no fight left in this young rooster," he said, contemptuously, and stooping, he cut the rope that bound the boy's hands and feet.

Tom staggered up, obedient to the pirate's order. With his uncle and aunt he was hustled out of the cabin and off the boat. They found themselves on a rough log landing stage in the shadow of a great bare wall of rock that shot straight up a hundred feet from the level of the water. In the face of this sheer cliff, and directly back of the landing stage, yawned a cavern. Its entrance, Tom thought, must be nearly ninety feet across, and half as high. It was arched like a broad, black doorway and most of its irregularities had been cut away, so that it looked more like the handiwork of men than of nature.

"Come on there, move along in!" shouted Rogers, and gave Tom a shove with his hand. The boy stumbled into the dark interior of the cave. He found himself in a chamber of rock a hundred feet or more in breadth, and at least forty feet high in the center. Far back in the depths of the cavern a light flickered deceptively. It might have been two hundred feet away, he thought.

Then, abruptly, the boy ceased marveling at the size of the cave, and turned his attention to a wholly different matter.

His aunt, his uncle and himself, together with the faithful Brad Bunker, had now been lined up against the wall of the cavern, a score of yards from the entrance, and Rogers was calling to someone farther within. "Come here an' hev a look at this passel o' prisoners!" he shouted.

Tom glanced back toward the river. There was one man in the entrance, stooping over a bundle of provisions. Tom was unbound. He could hear the steps of a party of men, approaching from the back of the cave. He thought he would never have a better chance than this. Free, he might still find a way to rescue his family. Without another second's delay he leaped toward the light and ran with all the speed of his long legs. But he had not counted on his faintness. Just before he reached the stooping man he stumbled and fell to his hands and knees. The pirate swung about at that instant, startled by a cry from Rogers, and before Tom could regain his feet the fellow had sprung on him and pinned him down.

For a moment Tom fought with the ferocity of a wildcat. He even succeeded in throwing his antagonist off and getting nearly clear, but his effort was in vain. The outlaws had run together quickly at the scream of the lame pilot and now they fell upon Tom, snarling like a pack of hounds.

Once more he was bound with ropes, hand and foot. When at last he lay quiet, the boy saw Jake Rogers standing over him, his eyes blazing.

"What'll we do with him, Jake?" panted one of Tom's captors.

The earless man spat viciously through his yellow teeth. "I'd gouge the eyes out o' the young devil if I had my way," he said, thickly. "Here—snake him back here an' let Jericho have a look at him."

Tom was half-dragged, half-carried for what seemed a long distance into the cave and flung down upon the ground. He saw that he was in a chamber not more than twenty feet square, hewn out of the soft rock and lighted by two fat tallow dips, set on a ledge. The floor of the place was cluttered with broken furniture, discarded clothing, empty bottles and a keg or two. In the midst of this jumble of odds and ends stood a rough puncheon table and about it four men were sitting, playing cards. Three of them jumped up when Tom was brought in, but the fourth sat quiet in his great chair cut out of a molasses hogshead. Tom knew that he was in the presence of Jericho Wilson and none other.

The man in the chair was vast and gross, a veritable mountain of flesh. His nose was long and bloated, and two great tusks of teeth in his lower jaw stood upward beyond his lip so that he looked, Tom thought, like a huge red boar. For red he was—red of skin and red of hair—with a growth of ruddy bristles on his jowls, and a rufous mat on his half-bare chest and arms.

He nodded to Rogers, at length, and spoke. His voice, beginning in a rumble, broke into a falsetto squeal.

"Howdy, Jake," he said. "Brung in a few, did ye! What in thunder was all that rumpus about?"

"Only this yere blasted pup tryin' to git away," replied Jake, indicating Tom with the toe of his hoot. "Second or third time he's give us trouble. What say, Jericho—kin I have him?"

There was something a little too casual in the lame outlaw's manner, as he spoke. Jericho's glinting pig's eyes studied his lieutenant shrewdly for a second. Then he answered, in a similar offhand way:

"No, Jake—guess we might's well keep him a while. Put him up garret. Won't be no trouble there."

Rogers tried to hide his scowl. "All right," he said. "There's three more outside—a woman an' two men. Good lot o' stuff they had—an' this." He flung on the table Ezra Lockwood's buckskin sack of money, and while Wilson and his three companions bent eagerly over it, the lean pilot motioned to the men with him to carry Tom out.

Half dead as he was with bruises and fatigue, the boy still managed to watch the preparations they made for disposing of him. The place to which he had been brought was at one side of the cave and still far to the rear—about fifty feet from Jericho's chamber, he judged. Two of the river pirates now came up, bearing between them a long ladder of poles, which they proceeded to lift, with a deal of swearing, and set against the sloping top of the cavern.

"Can ye see it?" one asked.

"No," grumbled his companion, "here—give us more light, somebody!"

A pine torch was brought and held aloft. Tom saw, dimly, in the flickering glow, a little hole in the cave's roof—a crevice, three or four feet long and half as wide. It was against the side of this dark opening that the outlaws finally leaned the upper end of the ladder.

"All right, up with him, now!" ordered Jake. Two of the strongest men took hold of Tom and started carrying him up the shaky poles. Once his dead weight of a hundred and sixty pounds caused the man below him to slip. Angrily the fellow secured a new hold, and they continued teetering upward.

At last they were at the top. One of his bearers held Tom against the ladder, while the other clambered out of sight through the hole. Then his arm came down and hauled the boy after him past the jaws of the opening.

As he was dragged into the pitchy darkness above, Tom's nose was instantly assailed by a heavy, nauseating smell. He fell back, limp and sick, too miserable for the moment to know or care what happened. Perhaps he even lost consciousness, for when next he began to take interest in his surroundings he discovered with some surprise that his bonds had been removed. Beside him, on the cold stone, his hand encountered a piece of the cord which the pirate had evidently cut loose and left there. A yard away a dim grayness showed the location of the hole through which he had been carried. Otherwise the place was as black as the inside of a pocket.

The boy sat up shakily and felt inside the breast of his buckskin top. It was there—the precious bit of a candle end that he had always carried for emergencies. The flint and steel in their little pouch were also discovered; and Tom struck a spark against the candle wick, nursing it into a tiny flame. Then he took the light in his hand and stood up.

The place in which he found himself was so huge that the feeble gleam failed to reach any part of its wall or roof. Here and there rose rough pillars of pale stone—stalagmites that had formed through endless centuries of time. They stretched upward for twenty feet and more and faded in the gloom. Something round and white on the uneven floor caught Tom's eyes and he moved toward it, not realizing till he was about to pick it up that the thing was a human skull. It was small—the skull of a child, he thought. But beyond it were other bones belonging to adult skeletons. They were scattered or in heaps, the remnants of many bodies, some covered still by rags of cloth.

The stench that rose from them nearly overcame Tom once more, and he turned away in stumbling haste. Ten paces off he came to one of the stone pillars. It was cold under his touch— dripping with damp. He snatched his hand away, and went on, but as he passed the big stalagmite, a looming, dark bulk on the floor behind it caused him to stop with a nervous catch of the breath. Whatever it was, the object had a square regularity of outline that soon reassured him. He stepped closer and the light glinted dully on moldy brass—the brass of a hinge.

The thing before him was a heavy chest of black wood, bound with metal. As he knelt to examine it something passed his head with a sudden swish, and the flame of his candle flickered and went out.

CHAPTER XIV

To Andy Warren, crouching beside the overturned dugout in the dark, the minutes that followed Tom's departure seemed to drag interminably. He could imagine his chum's slow and silent progress toward the outlaws' landing place, and the stealth with which he would reconnoiter their camp. But he knew, too, the danger that Tom ran.

Cub, the brown terrier, had been almost frantic in his desire to accompany his owner. Now the little dog lay by Andy's side, quiveringly alert, testing the wind from down the shore with ears and nose. It must have been close to half an hour after Tom left, that Cub rose suddenly, bristling but silent, his alert head cocked in the direction the boy had taken. Andy's hand clutched the hair on the dog's neck.

"What do ye hear, lad?" he whispered. Some sound, too faint for human ears, must have been borne upriver on the light, steady breeze, for at that instant the terrier stiffened and began to growl.

"Shet up, ye leetle divil!" Andy commanded. "Want to git us all kilt?"

The dog grew quiet, listened again, then turned to Andy, whimpering in pathetic eagerness, and would have dashed off down the shore, had not the boy held him fast.

Slow hours went by and Andy began to grow worried. He changed his position restlessly, many times. Tom should have returned before this. It must, he thought, be nearing dawn. At last he could wait no longer, but tied a thong of buckskin around Cub's neck, and holding the leash securely set out through the black woods.

The first dim light was on the trees when they came to the camp. Andy knelt in the brush, gripping Cub's jaws, and waited for what might come. The sun rose and figures appeared on shore above the keelboat. Preparations for the start were made. With laughter and yawns and curses the men cast off the mooring ropes and the *Phoebe Ann* drifted away on the swift, brown current.

Andy turned back with a heavy heart and retraced his steps up the shore. But it was not until he reached the dugout and found their little camp deserted, as he had left it, that he wholly gave up hope. Tom, he knew, now, had been killed or captured by the river pirates.

Lonelier than he had ever been in all his lonely life, Andy gathered an armful of driftwood and mechanically set about the preparation of a meal. There had been little sympathy and no real friendship in the redhaired lad's experience until that day on the river bank in Pittsburgh when he had first seen Tom Lockwood. From that hour he had worshiped the bigger boy. Now, as he thought of his friend, dead or a prisoner in the hands of the vengeful Jake Rogers, Andy's heart swelled within him and he got to his feet with a fierce resolve. He would go down the river and save Tom if he still lived, even though he would have to follow the outlaws into the cave itself.

There was a cold mist on the bank that morning. Shivering, the riverboy gulped down some food, launched the canoe, and with Cub sitting dejected amidships, paddled westward along the shore. He kept close in by the shadowy bank and moved slowly, for he knew that any plan he might make would be thwarted if the rivermen even suspected his presence.

It was late in the forenoon when he sighted the *Phoebe Ann,* half a mile ahead. The keelboat was already making over toward the northern shore for her landing. Andy paddled faster and came shooting down in the shallow water close to shore. A big tree trunk jutted out from the bank, two hundred yards or so above the cavemouth, and he brought his canoe to rest behind the screen of leaves that still grew along the fallen boughs.

From this point he could see with fair distinctness all that happened on the landing stage below. He watched the pirates make fast their prize and saw the bales and barrels carried ashore. Then a woman and a bearded man appeared on the gangplank, and following them a tall figure in ragged buckskin stumbled unsteadily toward the dock. It was Tom. He was alive! The prisoners were driven into the dark mouth of the cavern and the outlaws went on with their unloading.

Andy waited for no more, but turned and paddled quietly back upstream for nearly a mile. He wanted to make camp in some spot where he would be safe from discovery, and think things out. Coming to the mouth of a tiny stream, he put the bow of the canoe up it and paddled for a score of yards. The place was shadowed by big trees and behind it the bluff rose abruptly. Andy pulled up the dugout and sat down on a root to make a plan. He did not progress very rapidly at this, for the difficulties in his way seemed appalling.

At the entrance to the cave, as he well knew, a stout barrier was erected and a guard kept, night and day. He was considering the idea of openly entering the place as if he were still a member of the gang, and, if opportunity offered, helping Tom to escape, when a distant barking brought him to his feet with a jump. Cub was gone. Foolishly he had forgotten to tie him when he landed, and now the dog had run off in search of his owner. This might easily ruin everything. The boy gave a long, sharp whistle, and Cub barked again in answer. The sound seemed to come from above, at the top of the bluff. Andy ran toward the base of the hundred-foot precipice and looked upward. There was no path, but he saw that he could climb at least half the distance by holding to roots and outcroppings.

When he had scaled this first slope he came to a sheer cliff of rock, that rose thirty feet above his head, and offered no hold for foot or hand. He looked about despairingly. Cub must have gone some distance up the shore to find an easier ascent, and if Andy tried to do likewise the dog might start toward the cave and betray them both. He whistled again, and Cub replied with another series of barks. Looking up, Andy's eye fell on a tangle of wild grapevines growing at the top of the cliff. One of the vines, an inch or more in thickness, hung downward to a point four or five feet above his head and swayed, temptingly. Andy pulled out his hunting knife and started cutting at the soft stone of the cliffside. His blade was soon dulled but in a few moments he had made two or three rough indentations which his moccasins could grip. He drew himself up till his hand touched the grapevine and pulled on it strongly. The natural rope would bear his weight, he decided. Then like a cat he went upward, hand over hand.

At the top he found Cub waiting for him. The terrier seemed to have recovered some of his buoyant spirits, for he almost frisked as they went through the leafy undergrowth.

Andy hardly knew what direction they took. He had never before seen this country above the cliff, and he had a half-conscious interest in exploring it. But his mind was constantly busy with schemes for helping Tom, so that he followed Cub's lead more or less blindly. They had been progressing thus for perhaps half an hour when Andy missed the dog and called to him in a low tone. At first there was no answer. Then he heard a muffled, eager whine a little way off in the brush, and a moment after, Cub came leaping toward him. From his actions it was evident that the dog had found something. He ran back into the clump of thick undergrowth from which he had emerged, plainly wishing Andy to follow him.

The boy plowed his way through the branches and saw Cub scramble down into a hollow amidst the brush. Kneeling beside the depression, he leaned far over. The terrier was digging fiercely at a crevice in the rocks, his breath coming in frantic little whines. A faint, stale odor of decayed flesh reached Andy's nostrils. "Shucks!" he said. " 'Tain't nothin' but a ol' foxhole!"

Without knowing exactly why, he was disappointed. Perhaps he had felt some vague hope that Cub had discovered a back entrance to the cave—but no, that was too ridiculous. He started away, telling the dog to follow him. The terrier stayed, and still worked at this opening with his claws. Impatiently Andy returned.

"Here, dog!" he ordered, "Leave that and come with me."

But as he stooped to seize Cub's neck a tiny sound, scarcely audible, came to his ears. It was a noise no louder than the ticking of a watch under a pillow—a faint tack-tack-tack, regularly repeated.

With a gasp of astonishment, Andy fell to his knees beside the cranny, and started feverishly to remove the earth and stones.

CHAPTER XV

WHEN TOM had come to himself, after being left in the secret upper cave of the river gang, he had realized at once that his chances of escape were now reduced practically to nothing. Weak as he was with hunger, thirst and bruises, he could not hope to jump the thirty feet to the stone floor below and then fight his way out of the main cave.

As he explored his prison and discovered the skeletons of former inmates, it became evident to Tom that his captors almost certainly meant to starve him to death. Then, in the very act of staggering away from the gruesome heap of bones, he had come by chance on the great black box behind the pillar.

The sudden descent of the dark, as his candle was blown out, left the boy for a moment motionless with fear. He crouched on the damp stone, hardly breathing, until the realization came to him that the light had been extinguished by nothing more terrible than a swooping bat. And with shaky fingers he relit his candle.

Before him was the chest, ponderous with brass work and nails. A mighty padlock fastened its cover. There were leather loops for handles at each of the four corners, and Tom took hold of one of these, braced his feet, and put all his strength into an attempt to lift it. The box remained as solidly implanted as though it were a part of the stone floor. He held his light close, and examined both ends of the chest, then the back. And there, cut deeply into the old, dark wood, were letters—"R. W. of W." Tom puzzled over the inscription for a little, trying in vain to fit names to the initials. Then he pulled at the big padlock once more and felt of the woodwork appraisingly. Was this some part of the river pirates' treasure that he had found? A deep breath of excitement filled his lungs as he speculated on the possibility of such a discovery. But in the next instant the thrill went out of him as he remembered that in all likelihood he would never leave that vault of death. He set his candle end upon the chest and sank down wearily before it.

How long Tom sat there despondent he could not have said, but it must have been no great space of time, for there was still an inch of candle left when he looked at it once more. Dully his glance rested on the light for a moment. Then an odd thing caught his attention. The yellow flame of the dip did not burn steadily, and erect, but flickered constantly in one direction, as if swept by a draft. The flame was slanted, as Tom saw, *away* from the opening from the lower cave. Hastily he seized the candle and moved forward as the little blaze pointed, walking between the great stalagmites, with his eyes glued to the light. After he had progressed a hundred and fifty yards the direction of the flicker changed, and he followed again—this time four or five slow paces to the right. The flame burned straight upward. Tom moved about, a short distance each way, to make sure he had found the exact spot above which the draft made its exit. Close by was a stone pillar of odd, irregular shape, and the roof of the cave, evidently lower here, was dimly to be seen above.

Taking careful bearings, so that he could easily find the place again, Tom hurried back to the hole in the floor, and secured the length of rope he had found by his side after the outlaw had left. With this he returned to his strange-shaped pillar. The distance he traversed in reaching it was close to two hundred yards in all, and Tom realized that the upper cave must run back much farther into the bluff than the one below.

He studied the pillar carefully from all sides. It appeared to reach without a break from the floor to the roof above, evidently meeting and joining a stalactite, extending downward. Satisfied that he could remember the shape of the pillar in the dark, Tom passed the cord about its base and tied a firm knot. Then he blew out the candle and put it back in his shirt. The loop of rope gave enough slack to admit his body. He raised it as high as possible on the back of the pillar, worked his feet up till they gripped the rough stone, stood erect, raised the rope again, and so gradually ascended the stalagmite. Weak as he was the climb was achieved with comparative ease, for sitting in the bight of the cord he could rest when it was necessary. After perhaps a dozen pauses to readjust the rope sling, Tom knew he must be getting close to the roof. He stretched one hand as high as possible and felt a broadening of the stalactite, which confirmed his belief. Another hitch upward and he could feel the roughly level top of the cave. His groping fingers came to an abrupt upward curve in the limestone, a yard or less from the top of the column, and then, as his touch rested there, the boy drew a sudden exultant breath. A steady current of cool air was passing upward across his hand.

Spreading his fingers, Tom tried to gauge the breadth of the opening, but though it seemed to be over a foot wide at its base he judged that it must narrow somewhat, above. From the fact that no light came through he felt sure that the hole was long or very crooked, or possibly merely an opening into a third cave still higher in the bluff, and his moment of hope gave place to black despair once more when he remembered that he had neither tools nor strength with which to widen the passage.

By this time the rope was beginning to feel sharp and un-comfortable. Tom was preparing to begin the descent of the column when he thought he heard a faint scratching noise. He waited, straining his ears to catch the sound once more. After a moment of silence it came again, apparently above his head.

Could it be that some animal had its burrow in the passage he had just found? The scratching noise ceased for an interval, then was resumed, louder than before. And suddenly Tom heard a voice, very thin and far away, like a whisper coming through a horn. The words were indistinguishable except for one—and that word was "Cub!"

Tom dared not shout, except as a last resort, for he was not sure whether or not he could be heard in the cave below. Desperately he tried to think of a way to make Andy hear, as the precious seconds fled. He tried calling in a low tone but there was no answer. Then he remembered the bit of steel with which he was accustomed to strike a spark in making a fire. He pulled it out of his tunic with a shaking hand and, reaching up into the opening, began to knock with the metal on the limestone.

Cub began scratching again, above, and he heard Andy speak once more. Constantly he kept up his tap-tap-tapping on the rock, though his arm was very tired.

"Tom!" cried the voice above. "Just stay there, boy! I'll go an' git the ax an' see if I can't dig ye out!"

Tom tapped thrice, as hard as he could, for he wanted Andy to know that he had heard and understood.

After that his redhaired chum must have gone away for there was silence for a time, broken only by the occasional scratching of the faithful little dog.

Tom, uncomfortable as he was in the rope sling, stuck to his post at the top of the pillar. He did not know how far Andy would have to go for the ax, and was afraid that if he climbed down the other boy might return in his absence. So he clung there though his arms and legs were numb.

A time that seemed endless went by. At last Tom heard Cub whimper joyfully, and then the eager voice of his friend came down the rock chimney.

"Here comes sump'n fer ye to eat," called Andy. "Are ye

thar?" Tom thumped in answer and after a moment his hand felt something emerging from the passage above. He seized it, and to his joy found a cold roasted pigeon tied to the end of a stick. No food had ever tasted as delicious to Tom as that plump little fowl, eaten with one hand, in the pitchy dark.

Over his head as he munched he heard the steady clip-clop of the ax in the soft limestone. Chips began to tumble through the opening.

"All right, Tom, boy!" came Andy's voice after a while. "She cuts easy. I'm in more'n a foot a'ready!"

Tom's spirits had revived after eating the pigeon, but his cramped position was now becoming exceedingly painful, and he let himself down and lay on the cavern's floor to rest.

Above in the passage sounded the constant faint ring of Andy's ax. All of a sudden, as he looked upward, Tom saw a glimmer of white daylight, and a lump of rock bigger than his head tumbled into the cave. Andy's chopping ceased. "Are you there, Tom!" he called, cautiously.

"Here!" answered Tom, as loudly as he dared. "I climbed down for a rest. Wait a jiffy—I'm coming right up again."

Quickly he kicked the pieces of rock out of sight in a corner and reascended the stone column. As he reached the top he leaned far back and looked upward through the opening. It now disclosed itself as a crooked and uneven passage, four or five feet deep and a foot or more wide by twice as long. Something dangled against his hand and he took hold of it. At the same time Andy's delighted face half obscured the upper end of the opening.

"That's a piece o' grapevine I cut," said the riverboy. "Ef ye ain't put on too much flesh I reckon ye kin git up through here, now."

Tom grinned as he seized the vine with both hands. "If that's all that's needed, I'll come through a-flying," he answered.

By using the sling rope as a rest for his feet, he was able to reach up so far that his head was almost in the opening, and he was just about to kick loose and start climbing the grapevine when a shout echoed along the rocky corridors. Tom looked back hastily toward the crevice by which he had entered the upper cave, and saw the red flare of a torch, surrounded by moving figures. At that distance their words were unintelligible, but he knew they had not yet seen him. By a superhuman effort he hauled himself upward till his knees could find lodgement in the sides of the passage. It was a tight squeeze in some places, but he worked his way through with desperate energy, and at last, with Andy helping him, he crawled exhausted into the upper air.

"Quick!" he gasped. "Shove something over that hole—the light—they'll see it!"

Andy quickly stuffed the hole with branches and covered it with stones. "What!" he said, "Were they right arter ye, Tom?"

"Yes," panted the taller lad. "And we've got to run, Andy—for if we don't get out of here in a hurry they'll catch us yet!"

CHAPTER XVI

A MILE OF rough country lay between the cave and the place where Andy had hidden the canoe. If Tom's legs had not been braced by the feeling of liberty regained, it is doubtful if he could have made it. But the sight of Cub, beside himself with joy at this reunion, and the friendly lift of Andy's hand where the going was worst, helped to keep heart in the boy, and he stumbled on by sheer force of will till they reached the top of the bluff. There he lay for a little and rested, while his red-haired chum cut a twenty-foot canoe pole and sharpened it. When some of Tom's strength had returned, they descended by Andy's grapevine ladder, scrambled down the face of the lower bluff, and found the overturned dugout undisturbed.

It was now late afternoon. The boys did not dare to build a fire, but concealed themselves in the brush and waited for the coming of darkness. Andy found a few stale biscuits which he had made days before and these they munched as they lay in their retreat. A fierce thirst tormented Tom, for he had gone without water for twenty-four hours, and he found it next to impossible to swallow the dry bread.

Andy watched his friend's efforts till he could stand it no longer, and then, in spite of whispered pleadings from Tom to stay where he was, slipped from cover and ran toward the little stream.

He reached the bank, filled his hat with the clear water, and was starting to return, when a dry stick crackled suddenly not twenty yards away. At the same instant, from the direction of the river, a man's voice sounded in a laugh. Andy dropped flat on his stomach and wriggled backward into the bed of the brook.

Two men passed, following a sort of rough path down the riverbank. Both carried rifles, and one had a turkey slung across his shoulder. They must have been hunters from the outlaw camp, for their faces were dimly familiar to Andy. A broken fragment of their conversation drifted back through the quiet dusk.

"—Funny thing—boy gittin' lost that way so quick, wa'n't it?"

"Sure 'nough 'twas funny…Jericho…go through that upper cave with torches sometime…maybe miles an' miles."

The voices became indistinguishable and finally ceased, as the pair drew farther away. Andy refilled his hat, crawled up from the streambed once more, and sped back to his waiting chum.

"Did ye hear what they was sayin'?" the riverboy asked, as Tom gulped the cool water.

"Yes, they think I strayed off in the cave somewhere and got lost," answered the taller lad. "Gee, Andy, it's a good thing you covered up that hole."

Evening fell rapidly. When it had grown dark enough to travel in safety, Andy dragged the dugout down to the little stream and launched it. Tom felt so much refreshed after his rest that he insisted on taking a paddle as usual, while Andy used the long pole. Forcing the little craft up against the current was a fairly difficult task, but they kept steadily at work and at the end of two hours they had reached a tiny bay on the northern shore, four or five miles above the cave. There was dense cover along the bank and a good level spot for a camp, behind it. They unloaded their supplies, pulled up the canoe, and prepared for the night.

Tom, who was still hungry, suggested that they build a little fire and cook some meat. He stood erect and sniffed at the air. The wind was west and blowing softly up the river. The smoke would not be carried toward their enemies but away from them. Andy brought a big armful of dry wood and in a few minutes there were two pieces of venison broiling on the ends of green sticks.

The boys lolled on the clean grass, reveling in their first relaxation after the strain of the day's adventures.

"How!" said a deep voice. It was as sudden as that. Even Cub, worrying a bone by the fire, had failed to notice the presence of the new arrival until he spoke. Both Tom and Andy sprang to their feet, startled. There, on the opposite side of the blaze, stood a tall, blanketed figure, one bronzed arm held up in greeting.

"How!" repeated the native, and advanced a step.

"How!" returned the two boys, almost together, and Tom, who had recovered his composure, pointed to a place by the fire, and himself sat down.

The man took a sedate pace forward and seated himself in the spot indicated. For a long time he looked into the fire without speaking. Both Tom and Andy knew something of the native people's ways and they too preserved a dignified silence. At length, when the Pennsylvania boy started to cut a third piece of meat, the native raised his hand in a negative gesture.

"Wah-kee-tan has eaten," he said. Then, as the boys began to devour their own venison, the tall man spoke further.

"Wah-kee-tan is Shawnee," he said. "The settlers who come down the great water are his friends. But below are bad people, the men whose chief is Great-Pig-Living-in-the-Rocks.

"Wah-kee-tan smelled the fire and came to tell the young ones this."

The Shawnee paused, reached inside his blanket, and drew out a long wooden pipe and some dried leaves of tobacco. With great deliberation he crumbled the leaves in the palm of his hand and filled the pipe, then lit it with a coal from the fire. After two or three slow puffs he passed the symbol of friendship to Andy, who sat nearest him. The redhaired boy pulled soberly at the mouthpiece a few times, and handed the pipe on to Tom, while Wah-kee-tan began to speak once more.

"In the morning will come long knives from up the great water," he said. "Wah-kee-tan's canoe has passed their boat. They are as many as the suns between moon and moon. Wait and go with them, for the bad men cannot stand against the long knives."

The two boys exchanged a glance. "Buckeye Ben!" exclaimed Tom under his breath. Then he returned the long-stemmed pipe to the man and answered slowly, choosing his words.

"Wah-kee-tan has spoken well," he said. "The long knives are friends to us and to the Shawnees. Did Wah-kee-tan see the chief of these long knives?"

"He had on his head the skin of a wolf," replied the man.

"It is well," Tom said. "And were they in two boats?"

"All were in one long boat," answered Wah-kee-tan.

Tom nodded. "In the morning we will go to meet them," he said.

The man's lean, coppery face showed no sign of pleasure, but evidently he was satisfied, for at the end of a few moments he rose and went into the woods as silently as he had come.

When their guest was gone, Tom turned toward Andy eagerly. "That's the Muskingum hunters, sure!" he said. "But where's their other keelboat?"

"Mebbe lost her in the Falls," Andy hazarded, "though 'tain't likely. They had some good pilots in that crowd. Wal, we'll find out, come mornin'. What do ye figger to do—pole up a ways farther an' meet 'em?"

"Yes," said Tom, "I want to stop them before they get too close to the cave. If the outlaws don't know they're coming I've got a scheme, Andy—" and he launched into a whispered elaboration of his plan that made Andy's eyes shine with excitement.

After a council of war that lasted half an hour or more, the two lads doused their fire and went to sleep, leaving Cub on guard.

CHAPTER XVII

"Here, you long-legged loafer—wake up! Pancakes are a-fryin',
an' if you plan to feed before we starts you'd better roll out!"

Tom's eyes opened slowly and he saw Andy's face grinning
at him in the dim light of the early morning. The exhaustion
caused by his previous day's experiences had been swept away
by eight hours of solid slumber, and at the mention of breakfast,
Tom's ravenous appetite pulled him to his feet with a jump. He
went down to the bank of the cove, splashed his head and arms
into the cold water and returned to the campfire. Aside from a
little stiffness in his shoulder muscles, he felt as well as ever.

They ate quickly and in silence, and it was still before sunrise when they launched the little *Defiance* once more. Tom
picked up the pole and started shoving the canoe upstream
along the bank.

"You'd better swab out those rifles, Andy, and get 'em ready
for business," he said. "And if your knife's as dull as mine, they
both need whetting a bit. Reckon we might use 'em before we
sleep again."

The mist rose slowly off the water as they progressed up the
shore. Birds were singing in the trees close to the river. The
morning was bright with spring. The thrill of it got into Andy's
blood, and he hummed "Turkey in the Straw" under his breath
as he polished the long-barreled guns. Tom was no less keenly
alive to the beauty of the day, but he kept a careful watch on
the river, both before and behind them, and it was his eye that
detected the buckskin-clad figure of a man, in the shadow of a
tree, some distance up the bank. In a low voice, he told Andy
what he saw.

"All right," the redhaired boy answered, "I kep' one of 'em loaded a-purpose. Pertend ye don't see him an' keep a-goin'. Ef it's one o' Jericho's men he won't git the drop on me." So saying, he picked up the loaded rifle and held it ready below the gunwale. Slowly Tom poled the canoe up the shore. Out of the corner of his eye he constantly watched the spot where he had glimpsed the man. The figure disappeared for a moment, then came in sight again, this time in the sunlight at the water's edge. As Tom got a good view of the man's gigantic body and black bearskin cap he raised his arm in a gesture of greeting.

"Ahoy, Tom Lockwood!" boomed the great voice of B'ar Hanson. Tom drove the canoe over to the bank with a dozen stout shoves, and the big Muskingum hunter seized the bow, pulling them aground.

"You boys must be goin' back to Pittsburgh," he laughed. Then he noticed the sober look on Tom's face, and his hilarity gave place at once to seriousness.

"What's a-doin', Tom?" he asked.

"Trouble, I'm afraid," answered the boy. "We caught up with the *Phoebe Ann,* all right, but trying to get my aunt and uncle out of her I was nabbed myself. The Wilson Gang took me in their cave, and—"

Hanson leaned forward, staring. "You was in the cave—a prisoner—an' you got *out?*" he asked in astonishment.

"Thanks to Cub and Andy and a lot of luck, I did," said Tom, and he went on briefly to tell his story.

A delighted expression came over B'ar's face as he listened. "Here," he chuckled, at length, "come a-runnin'. We've got to let Ben know about this." And he led the way up the shore, talking as he went.

"The night arter you left us, up 'bove the Falls," he said, "we made B'ar Grass Creek, an' put in, waitin' fer daylight to shoot the rips. All but two of us went ashore an' took in the sights o' Louisville. Ye know, Colonel Dan'el Boone, hisself, was thar, an' he was 'quainted with Buckeye from the time he was a baby in the stockade at Harrodsburg. So we all sat 'round a-listenin' whilst Dan'el told stories about the ol' time in the Missoura country whar he lives now."

Tom looked at Andy with a long face as the recital progressed. "Jiminy!" he murmured, "Think of it, Andy—if we'd stopped in Louisville we'd have seen him, too."

"Wal," continued Hanson, "when we finally come back to the creek, thar was the two guards fast asleep on one boat. T'other boat was gone, 'long with half our provisions. Ain't but one gang on the river would ha' dared to do that. Buckeye Ben ain't sayin' much but he's sore all the way through. Fust his rifle, an' now his keelboat, an' him the leader o' thirty hunters! But Ben knows how all of us are itchin' to git to close holts with them downriver sneaks, an' I'm dead sure he's plannin' trouble for Jericho."

They had now come nearly half a mile from the place where they had left the canoe, and ahead they could see a light through the trees. In a moment Hanson led the way out to the shore of a deep, narrow cove.

Fifteen or twenty men in buckskin sat about on the bank, occupied in various ways. One was preparing a whole side of venison for cooking. Others were scraping hides, cleaning weapons, or fishing from the deck of the keelboat, tied closeby. They greeted the arrival of the boys with shouts, and someone called Buckeye Ben from the boat's cabin. When the chief had welcomed Tom and Andy with one of his rare smiles, B'ar Hanson beckoned him aside and spoke eagerly for a few moments. At one point in the conversation Tom saw the lean face of the hunter flash suddenly with interest. He called the boys to his side.

"You say there's a second cave above the one where Jericho's gang hangs out?" Buckeye Ben asked Tom.

"Yes," said the boy. "It runs back a long way into the bluff, and the hole I got out of is a couple of hundred yards from the opening that leads into the lower cave."

"And you don't think the rivermen know about the hole in the top of the second cave?"

"I'm sure they don't. It would be next to impossible to find it now that we've plugged it up, and I don't think they ever go up in the woods back of the cave. The cliff is too steep to climb easily and they do their hunting up and down the shore."

"How big are the two holes?" asked Chandler.

"Big enough for men to go through, one at a time," Tom replied. "With a rope, twenty men could get into the lower cave from the upper one inside of a minute."

Andy spoke up eagerly. "You see the only guards they keep are right at the front of the cave," he said. "Even if they was awake, they couldn't hear you comin' down through the trap, fer it's a long ways in. Jericho an' most of his gang sleep at the back an' along the sides, an' they sleep sound. Thar's allus plenty o' licker in that thar camp!"

Buckeye Ben had been listening attentively. Now he talked for a time with Hanson in an undertone. When they finished, both men walked toward the cooking fire. There was a glint in Chandler's eyes, and his strong teeth showed in a grin, as he called the hunters together.

"Tonight we go down the river," he said, when at length all were assembled. There was a murmur of delight from the bronzed woodsmen. Then he continued:

"These lads have shown us a way to take Jericho's varmints by surprise, and you wildcat eaters'll have all the rough an' tumble you want before mornin'. Everybody get some sleep if you can."

Horseplay and gleeful laughter followed this news. The men at once set about preparing their weapons. Some of them carried tomahawks and all had the great skinning blades that had earned them the name of "long knives" among the native people. Whetstones were called into service, powder horns and bullet pouches were filled, and the camp took on a general air of bustle.

After the noon meal, many of the hunters spread their blankets on the ground for a nap. Tom and Andy saw the good sense in this manouevre and did likewise, but while the Muskingum men snored away as peacefully as if nothing were in prospect, neither of the boys succeeded in dropping off until late afternoon. They must have slept for several hours, for it was dark when Tom awoke suddenly and sat upright. Around him the hunters' supper fire spread a cheerful glow. Meat was roasting on a long spit over the blaze, and the delicious odor of it filled the glade.

Deerskin hunting shirts and fringed breeches softly reflected the firelight. Near the middle of the group of lounging hunters, B'ar Hanson was dancing a clog that fairly shook the ground, his great arms swinging in ludicrous gestures and a mischievous grin lighting his broad face. Someone sang in a mellow, untrained baritone, and the woodsmen clapped their hands, beating time to the song and the dance.

Tom and Andy sprang up and went to join the crowd around the fire, laughing at the antics of their huge friend. It was just at this moment, when the merriment was at its height, that a tall figure stalked into the circle of the firelight. Wahkee-tan, the Shawnee, naked except for his loincloth, stood in the midst of the hunters. The Shawnee's face was streaked with daubs of black and red war paint. In his hand was a rifle, and at his side hung a tomahawk.

As if at a signal the place grew quiet. Hanson stopped his shuffling dance and raised an arm in greeting, for he evidently recognized the peculiar paint marks of the Shawnee tribe. The Shawnee returned this friendly salute, and when Buckeye Ben appeared from the other side of the fire, he turned and addressed the chief of the hunters.

"When the long knives go down to fight Great-Pig-Living-in-the-Rocks, Wah-kee-tan will go with them," he said. "There is a Huron among the bad men who is Wah-kee-tan's enemy." As he spoke he laid his right hand lightly on the haft of his tomahawk.

Buckeye Ben made a gesture of assent. "It is well," he said. "Come now, and eat with us."

But the gaunt Shawnee shook his head. "Wah-kee-tan will eat when he has killed," he answered simply.

The coming of the Shawnee seemed to have brought the hunters to a more serious realization of the work they had in hand. Grimly they ate their supper and quenched the fire. Then, while the keelboat was being loaded once more, Tom, Andy and Cub got into Wah-kee-tan's bark canoe, and with him set out downstream to pick up their own little craft. Five minutes' paddling brought them to the place on the bank where they had landed that morning, and they found the dugout without difficulty. The little company settled down on the shore to wait. The moon was not yet up, and a velvet darkness lay upon the river. A fitful wind blew from the south, shivering the leaves in the trees.

After a few moments the Shawnee pointed silently upstream. The boys could see nothing as yet, but the soft creak of an oar came through the dark and told them that the keelboat was drawing near. They launched their dugout, Wah-kee-tan knelt in his own canoe, and the two smaller vessels moved out to join the Muskingum boat. As stealthily as hunting owls the three craft swooped down with the current toward the den of the outlaw gang.

CHAPTER XVIII

THE WHITE DISC of the moon had pushed its edge above the hills astern and was flooding the valley with pale light when the little flotilla steered in toward the northern shore. The spot Buckeye Ben had chosen for landing his expedition was just above the small stream where Andy had previously camped. There, in the inky black shadow of a big pine, the keelboat was tied and the hunters paused for a whispered consultation. Eight of the best marksmen among that clan of born sharpshooters were picked by their chief to go down the riverbank afoot and station themselves near the cave mouth, in positions that commanded the entrance and the wooden landing stage. Wah-kee-tan volunteered to guide this detachment. "The Huron stands guard tonight at the cave door," he said, and a gleam came into his eyes, though the rest of his face might have been carved in oak.

The main force of the little army, numbering some twenty hunters besides the two boys, took its way upward in the direction of the bluff. B'ar Hanson carried a coil of rope, slung about his mighty shoulders. Some of the other men bore unlit torches of fat pine, in addition to their weapons. One by one the hunters ascended the cliff face, by means of Andy's grapevine ladder, and at the end of twenty minutes all stood safe at the top of the bluff.

Andy had attached the leash to Cub's neck, and as soon as the terrier understood what was wanted of him he set off at once in the direction of the place where Tom had made his escape.

Without the little dog's guidance the task of finding the hole would have been next to impossible. Only here and there did a level moonbeam penetrate the thick brush. For the most part the column stumbled forward through the darkness, each man blindly following the man just in front. The march through the forest consumed at least an hour, and it must have been close to midnight when Cub, tugging eagerly at his thong, brought Tom and Andy into the little hollow where instinct had first told him to dig for his young owner. Buckeye Ben and B'ar Hanson were close behind. They waited, talking in the faintest whispers, till all the hunters had drawn close. Then B'ar got ready his rope, putting a bend of it around a stout sapling near the hole. Tom stepped close to Buckeye Ben. "Let me go in first," he said. "I know the lay of the cave. If I see a light or hear any sound I'll give one jerk on the rope and you can pull me up. If things look all right I'll jerk three times."

Several of the hunters spoke up, anxious to make the first descent, but Buckeye agreed to let Tom reconnoiter. Slowly and with the greatest care the sticks and earth were removed from the aperture. When it was clear, Tom knelt and listened breathlessly. All was silent in the cave below. He took the two ends of the rope and let them down through the opening, then, leaving his rifle with Andy, he worked his way into the twisting passage. Descending, he found, was easier than climbing out. As his head followed his body into the cave, he paused, clinging where he was, and made a careful survey of the place. It was as black as a tomb, and as silent. He slid downward to the floor and waited in the stillness once more, then pulled three times on the rope. An answering tug showed that his message had been received. Almost at once the cord was shaken violently and another body dropped to the floor beside Tom. "Where are you?" came a whisper. "It's Andy. Shall I strike a light?"

"Better wait till they're all down," Tom answered. The hunters came through the opening in a steady stream, broken only when a bundle of rifles was let down, and again when B'ar Hanson's broad bulk stuck for a second in the passage. The big Muskingum man forced himself through with a mighty shove and descended, puffing, to stand with the quiet group on the cave floor.

For fear that Cub might bark, if left alone on the ground above, he too was let down, and at length Buckeye himself entered, pulling the rope down after him. As soon as the leader stood in the cave he struck flint and steel and lit a tallow dip.

The soft glow fell on a ring of tense faces and glimmered beyond them on the pale, rough stone. Chandler's level eyes, under the white wolf's teeth, moved slowly about the circle of his followers. Each man had now taken his rifle and stood in readiness. Buckeye Ben looked at Tom and gave a short nod. The boy turned at the signal, stepping silently in his moccasins along the cave floor, and led the way forward between the dripping pillars. When he came to the heap of bones he held up a hand in warning, then as the others paused he crept on, yard by yard, to the very rim of the opening. It gaped black there, below him, for there seemed to be no light in the lower cave. He leaned downward, listening, and caught at once the sound of the heavy breathing of many men asleep. Rising from his position above the hole, the boy went swiftly back to join the waiting hunters.

"All quiet down there," he whispered. "No lights lit, either."

"Good," said Buckeye Ben, softly. "We'll do it just as we planned, then. You wait till the last, and get these torches burning up here. Then down you come with the light, and we're ready for 'em."

Tom nodded, and at once set about lighting two of the fat pine splints from the candle, while the hunters gathered around the opening into the lower cave. Quickly the rope was passed around a stone column, and Andy, who knew the general shape of the cavern, slipped out of sight first, through the black hole.

After him, in swift succession, the hunters disappeared so silently that not even a tomahawk clinked on the stone. B'ar Hanson carried Cub, and another of the men took Tom's rifle. By the time the boy had brought the pine knots to a bright blaze, he found himself standing alone in the upper cave. A shiver of excitement passed through him, but as it passed he felt cool and steady. Everything was tensely quiet. He held the two burning torches in his left hand, took firm hold of the rope with his right, and gripping it below with twined legs, he started sliding downward. Five feet—ten—fifteen feet he descended, and a startled cry echoed through the cave. Tom slid faster at the sound, but by the time he touched the stone bedlam was let loose. There was a mighty answering shout from the Muskingum hunters, mingled with the fierce barking of Cub, as Hanson released his hold on the dog's muzzle.

Tom whirled about as he reached the floor, and held the torches in one hand, high above his head. Everywhere along the shadowy walls he saw startled figures leaping up. There seemed to be scores of outlaws in the dim place. Then all of a sudden, Buckeye Ben's voice rang clear above the tumult.

"Stand where you are and surrender or we fire!" he cried. His hunters stood in a grim, outward-facing circle, their ready rifles covering every cranny of the cave. The noise was hushed almost instantly, and sullen but helpless, the outlaws started to obey the order. Those who had seized weapons dropped them reluctantly. While Chandler detailed two of his men to gather all the outlaws' arms into a heap, Tom's eager glance was roving the cave in search of his family. He saw his uncle and aunt at last, sitting against the cave wall farther to the rear, their hands and feet bound. And beyond them, at that instant, something moved in the dark opening of the inner stone chamber. It was filled by a great bulk of flesh—the looming shape of Jericho Wilson himself. There was a tense second while the eyes of river pirates and hunters alike turned toward that menacing figure. Then Tom saw the quick flash of a raised arm, off at the left, and something flew through the air, striking the torches from his grip. As they fell, their light flickered out, and the blackness of the pit filled the place.

In the hurly-burly of the next few seconds Tom's only thought was to redeem his carelessness by recovering the smoldering pine knots and fanning them into a blaze once more. He fumbled about him on the floor, heedless of the trampling feet that seemed to be everywhere. The first yell of triumph had given place to a terrible, panting undertone, full of the hushed sounds of men groping, struggling in the breathless dark.

A wiry body lurched against Tom's, and hands laid hold of him, searching for his throat. The boy writhed half free, striking fiercely at the man before him, but long, lean fingers had twisted into the collar of his hunting shirt. He was yanked nearly off his feet before he could fairly grapple with his adversary.

"Huh! It's you, is it!" snarled a voice close to his ear, and cold despair entered Tom's heart as he heard it, for the voice was Earless Jake's. Vainly he tried to break the outlaw's grip. He knew that his strength was ebbing. Then a furry thunderbolt came through the air. Cub had leaped to his owner's defense. There was a worrying noise, and Tom's assailant let go his hold so suddenly that the boy stumbled forward to his hands and knees. His fingers came in contact with something that burned. He looked down, and there, still faintly glowing, was one of the pine torches. Tom seized the cool end, leaped to his feet and whirled the knotty splint rapidly about his head. Three times—four times—and the blaze burst out afresh, throwing its red glare over the wildest scene that Tom had ever beheld.

The battle filled the cave. Buckskinned hunters and motley rivermen were fighting everywhere, body to body and knife to knife. Only in one place, close to the wall and nearly opposite Tom, the struggle seemed fiercer than anywhere else. For a moment he could make out nothing more than a mighty tossing of bodies to and fro. Then there was an upward heave, and out of the maelstrom appeared the shaggy head of B'ar Hanson. A huge arm followed and the swarms of attackers were brushed away like flies.

And now there came storming through the cave a mountainous figure that swung a puncheon chair for a club, and left a swath behind like the track of a tornado. It was Jericho Wilson, the terror of the river, brought to bay at last. He let out a bass roar that ended in a squeal, and charged straight at B'ar Hanson with all the ferocity of a wounded boar.

That fight is talked of to this day among the old river captains —grandsons and great-grandsons of the men who saw it.

Wilson was the heavier of the two—they say he scaled close to three hundred pounds—but for all his bulk he was quick on his feet and a cunning fighter. From two paces off he hurled his crude weapon at B'ar Hanson's head and then dove in to seize him. The Muskingum man laughed, short and hoarse, and caught the chair in one big hand, smiting downward with it so hard that it broke in pieces on Jericho's shoulder. And then they were at it, bare-handed. Wilson had plunged for the hunter's waist and his momentum carried them both over and down with a crash. But Hanson, twisting as he fell, saved his head from striking the rock, and rolled from under his adversary. They surged to their feet at the same instant, and Wilson swung mightily with his fist at the backwoodsman's face. B'ar ducked, so that the blow only glanced from his temple, and stooping, he got a grip about the chest of the outlaw chief. Jericho wrenched to free himself, but those tremendous arms were locked. The riverman kicked and pounded at his opponent's body in vain. His breath was coming short now. He bent his great neck in a fruitless effort to bite Hanson's shoulder. At last his clawing fingers found their goal in the hunter's eye socket.

B'ar Hanson jerked his head from side to side to escape those desperate hands. A sudden frightful pain shot through his eye. He bowed his back yet more, his arms tightened, and there was a muffled cracking sound. Wilson uttered a great groan, as he tumbled in a heap on the ground.

All this had taken but a few seconds in the happening. Tom, still holding aloft the torch in his left hand, was defending himself with a tomahawk as he shouted encouragement to his big friend. Some of the outlaws who had tried to escape by the mouth of the cave had been met in the moonlight by deadly rifle fire, and such as were able had returned in haste. At the very instant that Jericho Wilson fell, Wah-kee-tan, terrible in his war paint, and eight tall hunters with leveled guns sprang into the circle of the torch light. The spirit went out of the rivermen at that sight. They were leaderless now, and outnumbered, and when Buckeye Ben lifted a bloody knife high above his head and once more called on them to surrender, the outlaws called for quarter on all sides.

The carnage ended. More torches were lit, weapons were piled in the center of the cave, and those rivermen who remained unhurt were lined up along one wall. There were only a bare dozen of them. Sixteen had been wounded more or less seriously, and ten were dead. Among these last was Jericho Wilson himself, for when they picked him up it was found that his back had been broken.

The casualties of the Muskingum men had not been so heavy. Only two of the hunters had been killed, though nearly every one had a knife wound or a battered head to show for the encounter.

Ben Chandler's orders crackled sharply through the cave. First the bodies were placed outside and covered with a great square of canvas. Then the wreckage of slab tables and stools was cleaned out and the prisoners made fast with heavily knotted ropes. In the middle of the line Tom saw the bloody but still sneering face of Jake Rogers.

The boy went straight to his uncle and aunt, and for a moment after he had cut their bonds the three clung together in speechless happiness. Then Tom's eye fell on Andy, standing awkwardly nearby, and he ran to his chum's side. Though the riverboy's fortune had been so closely interwoven with those of the Pennsylvania family, this was the first time that Ezra Lockwood and his wife had actually beheld him. The gentle Quaker lady saw blood staining the shoulder of Andy's shirt, and instantly she was all tenderness. Long before the last deft touch was given the bandage she had completely won the shy heart of the river lad.

Tom discovered Cub unconcernedly licking the dozen cuts and bruises that he had received during the fray. None of his wounds appeared to be very serious, and the terrier forgot them in a transport of joy, the moment he saw his owner.

A great weariness had settled over all the company. The hunters lay in little groups about the cave floor, and when Tom found a place to lie down, close to the entrance, nearly everyone around him was already asleep. Only the Shawnee, Wah-kee-tan, stood somber and tall, silhouetted against the night sky in the mouth of the cave. He raised his arms to the stars in some mysterious ritual of his people. From his girdle hung a fresh-cut scalp.

CHAPTER XIX

Tom Lockwood, never one to sleep long after dawn, was up and out before the others in the cave were well awake. He made a motion to rouse Andy as he passed him, but seeing the riverboy's tired face and remembering his wound he thought better of it. Cub, too, was snoring in doggy dreams. He would take his rifle, Tom decided, and go up the riverbank to see what game could be found for breakfast. There were turkeys, he knew, in the beech woods above the bluff. Partridges, of course, could be had almost anywhere along the shore, but he wanted if possible to bring back something bigger. As he stepped down upon the landing stage, the sight of Wah-kee-tan's bark canoe, moored to one of the piers, reminded him that his own dugout was still the best part of a mile up the shore. If he hunted upstream along the bank he could return by water.

When he had tramped half a mile or more through the green woods in the early morning light, Tom paused, listening intently, for he thought he had heard the distant gobble of a turkey up in the woods to his left. The faint sound was repeated after a moment, but before he had so much as taken a step, another noise, far louder, came from the river. It was a bass voice shouting the words of some ribald song. Where he stood, Tom was close to the water, and a lively curiosity drew him a few strides nearer the bank, where he could command a view of the stretch of river just above. Coming down rapidly with the current, close to shore, was a small flatboat, patched and shabby looking. There was something familiar about the craft. Tom was puzzling his brain to recall where he had seen her before, when a man's face, black-bearded and ugly, appeared at the rail.

With a violent start Tom realized that he was looking at Black Carnahan.

Even as recognition flashed through Tom's mind the boat had gone past. She was running a good six miles an hour on the strong current, and he knew well the roughness of the trail along the bank. Nevertheless he hauled his belt a notch tighter and set off down the shore at a long, swinging lope. Moment by moment he overhauled the broadhorn, which he could see in occasional glimpses through the trees to his left. Several men were on deck, now, and he thought he saw one make a gesture with his arm in the direction of the bank, lower down. Could it be that Carnahan meant to run in for the landing at the cave? The question was soon answered, for just as Tom came abreast he saw the steersman throw the tiller oar hard over, and the big craft began veering towards shore.

Tom's wind was still good. He bent low to avoid being seen, and ran his fastest. There were tangled berry vines in the path, but he went tearing through them, and the fallen logs that blocked his way he cleared in his stride. At last the high rock face of the cliff appeared ahead, with the broad opening gaping at its foot. Tom stole a look over his shoulder as he raced up to the entrance. The flatboat had not yet come in sight around the little bend, just above. The smoke of a breakfast fire was rising from the open space in front of the landing stage. Half a dozen hunters sat about it, and others were moving around in the gloom inside the cave mouth.

"Come in here, quick!" gasped Tom, with all the breath he had left. The men by the fire had jumped up at sight of the running boy, and they followed him into the cavern at once. Buckeye Ben hurried up. "What is it, lad—speak out!" he urged.

"Get your rifles," panted Tom. "Another boatload—Wilson's men—be here in a minute. If we keep out of sight—they'll land, sure!"

There was an instant scattering of the buckskin-clad woodsmen, to secure their guns, and in an incredibly short space of time the whole company was waiting, tense and ready, in the shadows along the cave wall. Tom found Andy at his side, rifle in hand.

"Who is it?" the riverboy whispered.

"Black Carnahan's crew," Tom replied. A gleam of satisfaction came into Andy's eyes and he crouched low, working forward until his eyes could command the landing stage.

At that moment there was a hail from outside, and the waiting hunters heard the creak and grind of the broadhorn's planking against the piers.

"That'll do," came Carnahan's hoarse bellow. "Now another turn o' rope around that post an' we'll be fast."

"Here they come," whispered Andy. All eyes were turned toward Buckeye Ben, who now raised his hand and motioned toward the entrance. Tom saw that the leader of the Muskingum men had recovered his stolen rifle. "Ol' Sal" lay once more in the crook of his arm. The hunters moved forward, every man with his rifle ready, and stood all across the cave mouth in a quiet line. The rivermen, some of whom had advanced already as far as the fire, were taken so utterly by surprise that for a moment none of them moved. The sight of that grim rank of rifles seemed to paralyze them.

Then Chandler's cool, crisp voice cut the silence suddenly.

"Hands above your heads and march up this way!" he ordered. They obeyed mechanically, and the two or three who had been carrying guns dropped them on the ground. There were eight or nine men in the huddled group that came forward to surrender.

"Hol' on a minute—Carnahan—whar's he?" cried Andy, as he searched the faces of the prisoners.

A sudden thudding of feet aboard the broadhorn answered him. Through the thin smoke of the fire, the boys glimpsed a stocky figure that leaped across to the deck of the *Phoebe Ann*, moored next below, and running the length of her side-planking, disappeared over the bow.

Tom and Andy, with half a dozen hunters at their heels, reached the landing stage within ten seconds after the fugitive dropped from sight, but to their astonishment, when they looked into the water over the keelboat's side, he seemed to have vanished completely. It was Tom who chanced to look down river and saw Carnahan, in the birch canoe, already fifty yards away and paddling like mad. Some of the hunters opened fire at once, though the mottled canoe, flashing through the shadows of trees close to shore, offered a poor target. Then Ben Chandler's voice rang clear in an order.

"Wait!" he cried. "We'll take him alive. Get a boat ready to follow him." And stepping through the group of hunters in the bow of the keelboat, the Muskingum captain raised his rifle, sighted with more than his usual care, and pulled the trigger. The amazed watchers saw the slender blade of Carnahan's paddle split cleanly in two pieces and fall from his hands useless, and as they realized what Buckeye Ben had done they raised a cheer that fairly shook the deck. Several of the hunters ran to launch a skiff, moored at the lower end of the dock, but even as they went they saw Carnahan stand erect in the canoe, look back, and throw himself into the turbulent brown water. Every one stood still, waiting for the man's evil head to break the surface again. A full minute passed and still he did not reappear.

"I recollec' now," said Andy. "He didn't know how to swim."

Slowly the hunters retraced their steps to the cave and preparations for breakfast were resumed. Needless to say, neither Tom nor Andy failed in his duty to the hot, brown buckwheat cakes that Mrs. Lockwood was frying. As Tom finished his tenth he turned to his redhaired friend. "Huh!" he said, "I clean forgot the turkey I meant to bring in for breakfast. Want to try the shooting up the shore, Andy?"

The riverboy was enthusiastic. "You bet!" he grinned. "I'm ready to start right now."

Tom looked around for Cub, and saw the terrier lying near the entrance with his scarred head on his paws. "Better let him rest," Andy said. "He fought like three dogs an' a catamount, last night."

Half a mile upstream, Tom turned to the left. "I heard a gobbler back here somewhere this morning," he said. "Let's try it."

There was a break in the wall of the bluff at this point, and a rough ravine, filled with a tangle of undergrowth, ran back into the forest. They made their way through the vines and brush and climbed at length into an open, shallow valley where the early sun struck in among budding beeches. Their moccasins made no noise on the soft ground as they moved slowly up the glade. At length to their intent ears came the sound they had been listening for—the faint *gobble-gobble* of a wild turkey —somewhere beyond a little ridge, to their right. Quietly the boys separated, crouching low to keep behind the cover, waited till they heard the sound once more, then wriggled forward on hands and knees to the top of the rising ground. Beyond, a hundred and fifty yards off, and feeding slowly nearer among the trees, were four turkeys—a gobbler and three hens. They blended so perfectly with the bronze and green of the woods that even Tom's keen eye could distinguish them only when they ran.

He looked over to the left for Andy, but the riverboy was out of sight behind some brush. Carefully he brought his rifle into position and waited, minute after minute. Finally the great gobbler came strutting into full view in front of a fallen log, and Tom fired. Almost instantly followed the report of Andy's gun. One of the hens rose on thundering wings and another scuttled into the bushes. Two heaps of ruffled feathers lay beside the log. With simultaneous yells, the two boys broke cover and raced to the spot where the turkeys had fallen. While Andy was reloading his rifle, Tom picked up the birds and tested their weight gleefully. Each of them weighed over fifteen pounds—the gobbler nearly twenty-five, he would have judged.

"Most 'nough meat thar to feed the whole camp," laughed Andy.

"Yes," said Tom, "if we could only get a little something else, now—a couple of squirrels, say, or—hark! What's that?"

Sharp and clear and at no great distance, they heard the barking of a dog. "It's Cub, and he's treed something, sure!" chuckled Tom, and picking up his gun and the turkey gobbler, he led the way in the direction of the sound.

As the boys scrambled through the tangle of undergrowth, there came a sudden change in the tone of Cub's bark. "Trouble!" said Tom, plunging forward at a run. He burst through a screening thicket and almost fell over a whirling mass of soft black fur and bristly brown hair. The terrier was in full combat with a quartergrown bear cub.

"Here—ketch holt an' loose 'em—mebbe we kin keep the leetle feller fer a pet!" cried Andy. But it was already too late. The dog had obtained a grip on the neck of his adversary, and a few savage jerks of his head sufficed to break the young bear's spine.

Now, suddenly, another actor came upon the scene. Out of the brush a dozen yards away crashed a black bear that looked as big as a house to the boys. She was still gaunt from her winter fast, and her little eyes glowed as she charged down upon the luckless dog. Cub dropped his victim and sprang adroitly aside, but the mother bear whirled almost as quickly. Her vengeful paw cut four red ribbons out of his flank.

Tom's rifle was already at his shoulder when in a sudden flash he remembered that he had not reloaded it after shooting at the turkey. He threw the weapon down in disgust, and tugged his hunting knife loose from its sheath.

The big bear, turning from the terrier, nuzzled once at her dead cub, then swung about to face the boys. She rose on her hind paws, half erect, and her lean black head swayed wickedly as she shuffled from one foot to the other. Andy's rifle was leveled at her breast. He took a cool and steady aim, but at the instant he pulled the trigger the big brute dropped on all fours. The crash of the report was mingled with a yell of pain from the bear, for his bullet had ripped searingly along her shoulder and side.

Maddened by the wound, the huge animal plunged forward, straight at the riverboy.

CHAPTER XX

IN THE SCANT SECOND that intervened between the firing of his rifle and the charge of the wounded bear, Andy drew his knife. She came on, striking fiercely with both forepaws. He thrust for her body with all his might but the blade was knocked out of his hand and when he tried to dodge backward, the great brute followed quicker than he could jump.

Tom, running in on the other side, saw his chum spin and fall as one of those tremendous paws caught him in the ribs. Then, as the bear plunged after her victim to finish him, Cub returned to the fray.

Like a small brown whirlwind the terrier flew at her flank, chopping deep with his keen, white teeth. The she-bear gave a sort of breathless snarl and whirled half about to meet the dog's attack. And Tom, leaping close in a single stride, drove his long blade home to the guard in her exposed side, just back of the left foreleg. The great beast coughed, lurched forward, stumbled and lay still.

Tom pulled his knife loose, looked to make certain that the bear was dead, and turned to help Andy. There, to his amazement, kneeling beside the lad, was a hunter in buckskin. Where the man had come from Tom could not imagine. He rose now, and turned a keen blue eye in the Pennsylvania boy's direction.

"Not a rib cracked," he said, cheerfully. "Wind all knocked out, that's all." And at that moment Andy confirmed the diagnosis by sitting up and beginning to breathe in hoarse gasps. He, too, looked up at the figure in buckskin with evident astonishment.

The hair beneath the man's squirrel-skin cap was almost snow white, yet he did not seem in the least decrepit. He was above the medium height, sturdily built and active, and he carried his massive shoulders splendidly erect. The skin of his face was weather-beaten to a leathery brown and criss-crossed with fine lines like the skin of a mellow russet apple. His features were rugged and strong, but the twinkling blue eyes, with crow's feet around their corners, gave him a kindly, almost gentle expression.

He nodded now at Tom. "Ye stuck that ol' b'ar about right," he said. "Better'n I managed with my first b'ar." As he spoke he stooped above the heap of black fur. "Goin' to skin her?" he asked.

"Yes, sir, I'd like to," said Tom, "only it's a long job, isn't it?"

"Oh, not so desp'rate long," chuckled the old man. He squatted by the bear's head and took from his belt a knife with a blade a foot in length which he proceeded to whet lightly on the heel of his hand.

"Ought to have her strung up, to work real fast," he continued, as he began to make deft incisions in the hide. "But takin' her warm, this way, she'll peel out right smart."

Cub, still bleeding and battle weary, limped up beside the stranger and sniffed at the fresh carcass, wagging his stump of a tail.

"Mighty good little dog o' yourn," said the hunter. "He pitched in when he was needed the most. There's a plenty without that much grit." He spared a hand from his work long enough to bestow a friendly pat on the terrier's head.

As soon as Tom had rebandaged Andy's wound, which had been opened when the bear struck him, both boys came forward to give what assistance they could in the skinning operation. But to their amazement they found the bear's body already stripped of its hide. The old woodsman was humming contentedly to himself while he cut the haunches and flanks into pieces suitable for carrying.

"Now then," he said, as he finished, "we'll make two-three leetle packs out o' this meat, an' see 'bout totin' it back to the river. You boys got a camp 'round yere?"

"Down below, at the cave, with Buckeye Ben's men," Tom answered.

"What—Ben Chandler? At Jericho Wilson's cave? What's he a-doin' in that sink hole?"

"We cleaned it out last night," said the Pennsylvania boy, proudly.

"Good enough!" exclaimed the old hunter. There was a gleam in his blue eyes. "That Wilson gang met up with their match at last, eh? Yes, Buckeye Ben, he's a good lad, an' a good shot. I'd liked to ha' gone to that party myself."

Andy and the stranger had picked up the packs of bear's meat during this conversation, and as soon as Tom had rolled up the heavy pelt and shouldered it they set out single file toward the shore. Coming to the fallen log where they had shot the turkeys they added the two big birds to their loads, and proceeded. Tom told briefly of their adventures on the river, as they went along.

"Come from Bucks County, eh?" the old man put in, eagerly. "Why, I was born in Berks, right next door, ye might say, an' my folks was Quakers, too. We moved to Virginny when I was a youngster, an' then down into the Yadkin valley, in Caroliny. When I was a man grown I crossed over into Kaintuck by the Nollichucky Trace.

"Hmm!" he mused, "there was b'ars in plenty on the river in those days."

"I should think so," Tom exclaimed. "Why, you must have come over the mountains back in the time of Harrod and Boone and General Clark!"

The white-haired woodsman shot a keen glance at Tom from his twinkling eyes. "Well—yes," he nodded, " 'bout that time, it was."

They had come out upon the bank, now, and saw, a short distance upstream, a small, well-built keelboat moored to a tree. Not above a score of yards farther on their own dugout lay on the bank, where they had left it the night before. Five or six hunters in deerskin were sitting on the deck of the keelboat, and these greeted the boys in friendly fashion when their new acquaintance led them aboard.

"We're goin' down river ourselves," he explained to Tom, "an' we'll set ye ashore at the cave. Maybe we'll even stop over for dinner, seein' as ye've got plenty o' fresh meat."

The canoe was tied astern, the mooring rope was cast off, and as the keelboat edged out into the current, the venerable hunter and his guests made themselves comfortable on the narrow afterdeck.

"Now," he said, turning toward Andy, "how 'bout this yere redheaded young bobcat, that b'ars can't kill?"

The riverlad reddened bashfully under his freckles. "I'm jest Andy Warren, from the Falls o' the Ohio," he mumbled.

The old hunter leaned forward, looking at him closely.

"Hold on!" he exclaimed. "Andy Warren—hmmm—was your pappy Dick Warren, the pilot?"

"He was that same," answered Andy with pride.

"Why, then you're the leetle tad I used to see 'round the tavern at Louisville, years ago, 'fore I went on West. I knew your father mighty well, boy. He was a man as straight as he was brave, an' he wasn't afeared o' nothin'. What troubles he had, an' they was a plenty, come on him through no fault o' hisn."

The old woodsman paused and when he spoke again his voice was curiously husky.

"I pulled him out o' the river once," he said, "an' he give me a knife to remember him by—the one I used today."

Andy started up in open-mouthed astonishment. "Why—why—you must be Colonel Boone!" he cried.

"That's what I'm called, sho' 'nough," smiled the hunter.

"Maybe you've heard your pappy speak o' me, then?"

Andy, suddenly tongue-tied, could only nod his head vigorously, while Tom whispered again and again, beneath his breath, "Daniel Boone—Daniel Boone, *himself!*" His mind could hardly encompass the tremendous fact that he sat in the presence of the great pioneer who had been a legendary hero to him ever since he was big enough to hold a rifle.

He—Tom Lockwood—had killed a bear in such fashion as to earn the praise of the most famous hunter in America! He pinched himself to make sure he was not dreaming.

They were already approaching the cave landing. The old frontiersman pulled from its sheath the long-bladed hunting knife and passed it to Andy.

"See thar?" he said. "Your pappy cut his initials on it."

Andy took the knife and examined it eagerly. "That's right," he said, "Richard Warren of Warrenton—R. W. of W.—that's what he was always carvin' on things."

Tom swung toward Andy so suddenly that he nearly lost his balance. "What did you say? What were those letters? Let me see!" he exclaimed.

Andy laid the knife in his hand. There, cut deep in the old, worn, wooden handle were the same initials he had seen, not forty-eight hours before, carved on the great black box in the upper cave.

CHAPTER XXI

Tom handed the knife back to the old hunter with fingers that trembled, and turned a flushed face toward Andy. But at that moment the side of the keelboat creaked along the log piers of the landing and in the midst of a general hullabaloo the Missouri hunters made her fast. The Muskingum men meanwhile ran down with whoops and yells to welcome their guests. In the tumult Tom managed to pull his chum out of the circle that surrounded Colonel Boone, and led him into the cave.

"Come here, Andy, quick! There's something I want to show you," he whispered and his voice was hoarse with excitement. "Have you got a piece of candle with you? Then come along!"

Running to the rear of the cave, Tom picked up one end of a long pole ladder—the same that the outlaws had used—and with Andy's help set it in place against the edge of the opening in the roof. They swarmed up the rungs like a pair of frightened cats and tumbled out upon the dark stone floor of the upper cavern. Tom had struck a light almost before Andy was upon his feet. With a glance around to make sure of his bearings, the Pennsylvania boy led the way rapidly past the white heaps of bones, and among the stalagmites till he came to one of the biggest of the stone pillars.

There he stopped and held his candle low, and Andy, stumbling close behind, saw a metal-bound chest, that loomed dark and mysterious in the uncertain light.

"Did you ever see that before?" Tom asked.

Andy shook his head. "No, not to remember, anyhow," he whispered.

"That's right," Tom replied, "you weren't much more than a baby—well, look at this, then."

Bending over the back of the chest as his chum held the candle down, the Kentucky boy read the letters "R. W. of W.," carved plainly and in a character he knew. For a moment he stared at the initials open-mouthed. Then he straightened up, his face flushed a dull red. "So 'twas Jericho Wilson as robbed my Pappy!" he muttered. "Wal, Jericho's done got his pay fer it, anyhow."

He put a hand in one of the leather loops and started to lift a corner of the box. It did not budge an inch.

"Why, it—it—*ain't empty!*" stammered Andy.

"No," Tom laughed, "it looks to me as if 'twas full. Only how are we going to prove it?"

At that moment a sound of voices echoed along the corridors of the cave, and the light of a torch appeared near the aperture through which the boys had climbed.

"Hello—Tom Lockwood!" came a hail.

"Right here, Uncle Ezra," Tom answered, recognizing the voice, and he stretched his hand with the candle aloft, to guide the steps of the approaching party. In a moment Ezra Lockwood, accompanied by Boone, Chandler, B'ar Hanson, and a number of others, had come up to the two boys and were examining their discovery with considerable astonishment.

"That's Dick Warren's, right enough," Daniel Boone pronounced. "He's told me of it more than once.

"Boy," and he turned to Andy, "I shouldn't wonder if you was rich."

All efforts to open the chest were unavailing, till at length one of the hunters brought a heavy crowbar from the lower cave. A few hard blows with the point of the bar shattered the lock. With a trembling hand Andy pulled it from the staple and threw back the cover of the box.

At first Tom, peering over Andy's shoulder, was disappointed because no sudden gleam of precious metal dazzled his eyes. Then he saw that the chest was filled nearly to the top with small brown canvas bags. Andy reached in gingerly and lifted out one of these. And as he untied the drawstring, a shower of silver and gold coins rolled out on the stone floor.

The money was counted and returned to the sack, and half a dozen other bags when opened revealed contents of a similar nature. As nearly as could be estimated, there was something over $40,000 in the chest.

That night there was a barbecue at the cave mouth. The light of a huge bonfire shone high up the cliff and cast its ruddy reflection on the river. Bear steak and roast turkey went the rounds and cider casks were broached. One of the Missouri men produced a clumsy-looking instrument that he called a cornstalk fiddle, and to its squeaking strains B'ar Hanson swung his great arms and danced thunderously on the keelboat decks.

It was the last evening that the company would be together. Ezra Lockwood, eager to reach his new home and break sod for the crops, had decided to start at sunup in the *Phoebe Ann*, Buckeye Ben's men had some repairs to make on the boat that they had recovered, and would follow a day or two later with the prisoners, turning them over to the authorities when they reached St. Louis. Boone wished to make an excursion into Illinois, to visit some old friends of his.

Tom and Andy sat a little apart from the uproarious group about the fire and talked of the many things that had befallen them in those last hectic days.

"Jiminy!" said Tom with a chuckle, "it was pretty lucky they put me up in that black hole of an upper cave, after all, wasn't it? Finding your father's box, I mean. And you know the funny part of it is, I'd probably have gone on clear to Missouri without ever thinking of it again, if Colonel Boone hadn't shown us that knife."

Andy was silent, energetically rolling the delighted Cub on the ground between his knees. Finally he looked up, reddening with embarrassment.

"Half o' that money's yourn, Tom," he said, and began rolling the dog again, harder than ever.

"That's sure mighty nice of you, Andy, and I appreciate it," answered Tom seriously. "But honestly I wouldn't know what to do with it. Money doesn't count for much where we're going. Uncle Ezra's got plenty to keep us till we have a house built and a harvest in, and after that we'll get along fine. Besides, they say there are more deer and turkeys in that Missouri country than here, even."

Andy paused once more in his furious game, and sat looking at Tom while the dog worried his moccasin.

"Wal," he began slowly, "I got it figgered out what I want to do with my part. Ye see I ain't never learned to talk nor read good, nor nothin'. I been jest a roustabout, spite o' my pappy bein' a gentleman. I'm goin' to take that money an' go back East to a college, an' when I'm eddicated I'll come down the river again."

"Andy," said a voice just behind the two boys, "you're doin' exactly right." And the big figure of Daniel Boone settled quietly down in the space between them. The old hunter put a hand on the shoulder of each, as he began to talk, looking off at the black, westward-hurrying river beyond the firelight.

"Yes, you're right, Andy, and Tom's right, too. Money don't cut much of a swath in that country up the Missouri. But book-larnin' does, and it will, more and more. You kin ride along through the woods in Missouri an' come on plenty o' tidy log houses, with gardens an' chickens, an' maybe an apple orchard if the folks have been thar long enough. An' you'll say, 'Wal, looks like a feller kin hold his own here an' be happy if he's got a rifle, an' an ax, an' a hoe.'

"Then right soon you'll happen across a place whar there's six or eight young uns a-playin' 'round the doorstep. An' it'll come to you all of a sudden that this country's growin' fast, an' gittin' full o' folks. What with the good ground, an' thousands o' families comin' down the Ohio year after year, thar'll soon be leetle schools an' churches an' towns a-springin' up.

"Already, in the country across the Mississip' thar's some biggety young men that want the western settlements to run theirselves, without any meddlin' from the President or Congress. An' in ten, or maybe a dozen years from now, thar'll be hundreds of 'em. If the folks in Missouri an' Illinois don't have men with brains an' judgment to lead 'em, they'll make some fool mistakes. They'll need men who can look way ahead, far enough to see what this country can grow into if everybody pulls together."

The old man rose and spread his great arms to east and west. A light was on his face brighter than the glow of the fire. "The people that have come to live in these valleys," he said, "are own kin to the folks back in Virginny an' New England an' the rest o' the states—brothers, sisters an' cousins. Some came an' some stayed. An' all this land, from the Lakes down to the Gulf is ours—America. It can be—it's *goin'* to be the greatest country in the world."

The stern light left his eyes as he concluded. He returned to sit once more between Andy and Tom.

"Ye see," he said, after a little, "I'm gettin' along past the age when I'll see much o' this myself. Reckon I wa'n't cut out fer that sort o' livin' anyhow. But you boys'll see it, an' be part of it. So, Andy, that's why I say you're right to go East an' git some schoolin'.

"But, sho'!" went on the white-haired hunter, "ye needn't to worry about that yet awhile. Come fall, ye kin go down to New Orleans, an' git aboard a packet bound for Baltimore or Philadelphy, an' make the whole trip in less'n a month. An' long 'fore the time comes to start, ye'll be a full-fledged Missourian.

"You boys have got some great sights ahead o' ye," he chuckled. "There'll be the ol' He-River, runnin' a couple o' miles wide, slow an' yaller. An' you'll go up, polin' along for days on end. An' you'll see prairie, stretchin' away, green an' rollin' without a sign of a tree, clear to the far aidge. You'll shoot your first buffalo, an' watch the herds of 'em run, with their tails up an' their heads to the ground an' their eyes shut, while the earth shakes.

"Yes," he repeated, a trifle sadly, "you'll see a heap o' things. Wish I was your age, an' goin' with ye."

CHAPTER XXII

IT WAS MORNING, and a slant ray of early sunlight caught the top of the little mast aboard the *Phoebe Ann.* The crossbar, formerly the perch of Jake Rogers' redoubtable coon, was no longer there. In its stead fluttered a wisp of starred bunting, bright-hued. Daniel Boone's keen old eye lit on it as he shook hands with Tom in farewell.

"That's the stuff, boy," he nodded, eagerly. "Ye put that up this mornin', didn't ye? Carry that flag up the Missouri! They need more of 'em up thar."

The partings were over. Andy and Tom caught the mooring ropes as they were flung aboard. Standing on the afterdeck of the *Phoebe Ann,* they watched the figures of their friends on shore grow smaller while the craft gathered speed in the current. Some hunter started singing, and as more and more Muskingum men took up the refrain the voices came strong across the water—

> "It's spring high water in Pittsburgh town,
>   Oh, high, O-hi-o!
> Lay her nose with the current an' let her run down,
>   Oh, high, O-hi-o!
> Down the big river an' west by south—
> To the Falls o' the Ohio, an' the Wabash mouth—
> For it's high water now, but there's gwineter be a drouth—
>   Down on the O-hi-o!"

The last line of the song echoed down the valley, and the boys saw B'ar Hanson, standing high on the bank by the cave mouth, wave his great bearskin cap in a final gesture of good-by. As the keelboat rounded the bend, they turned their faces to the west.

The Ohio seemed mightier than ever now, running deep and strong between the wooded banks. Half a dozen miles below the cave, the green head of an island rose, dividing the stream into two swift-running channels. Andy turned as he caught sight of it, and called to Ezra Lockwood, who had the stern oar.

"Watch out fer squalls, 'long here," he shouted. "This yere's ol' Hurricane Island! They's allus a thunderstorm or a gust o' wind waitin' to jump on ye when ye git past the p'int."

They swung into the left hand channel and at that moment, as if to prove the truth of Andy's words, a muffled *"bang!"* came to their ears.

"Wait a minute—that's not thunder!" said Tom, listening intently. Then, as the sound was repeated, "It's shooting!" he cried. "Someone firing guns, 'way up near the cave."

They strained their ears to catch the noise again, but no more of the reports reached them. "Most likely one o' them Muskingum fellers blazin' away at a turkey or a deer," suggested Andy. And they turned their attention to the wonders that were unfolding ahead of them.

Southward and westward they ran, all day, and the *Phoebe Ann* seemed magically to have crossed the line into another climate, for the sun fell with tropic warmth, and on the banks hundreds of wild fruit trees showed their massed white and pink blossoms amongst the rank green foliage of the forest.

They made their fifty miles that day, and camped, at nightfall, on a low, grassy island that lay along the inner side of a great curve in the river.

Next morning the keelboat was off to an early start once more. Some time in midmorning the voyagers saw the broad mouth of the Cumberland, and before dusk had fallen they passed the confluence of the Tennessee with the Ohio. Their anchorage that night was close above the little settlement at Paducah.

A mounting excitement possessed the boys as the third day wore along. They stayed together near the bows all afternoon, looking out ahead with expectant eyes. But still the river wound westward, and a light spring rain, that sheeted the banks with gray and brought the early darkness in its wake, caused Ezra Lockwood to drop anchor a little before the usual time.

Andy stood to windward of the supper fire and sniffed eagerly at the rain-soaked air that drifted up from the south and west. "Seems to me," he said judicially, "seems to me I can smell her already. Yessir, I b'lieve the ol' Mississip' is jes' down thar round the bend."

"What's she smell like?" Tom asked.

"Oh, mud," exclaimed Andy, "an' catfish, an' clamshells, besides a smell that's jes' the river, an' nothin' else."

Tom regarded his friend with a slightly incredulous smile, for though his keen nose had tested the air half a dozen times, he could find nothing unusual in the odor of the wet spring night.

But Andy was right. The *Phoebe Ann* had been in motion hardly an hour, next morning, when the river seemed to widen in the mist, before them. Somewhere overhead, the sun was shining, trying to break through the pall of smoky white that covered the water. The current had grown perceptibly slower.

"Time to get out the poles," said Andy, and as he spoke the fog began to separate and lift in wreathing spirals, and the sun shone on an immense reach of water, ahead of them and on either side. Dimly, a far-off shore became visible. They had come to the Father of Waters at last!

"Here, you lubber, look alive!" shouted Andy, as he thrust a long pole into Tom's hands. "Do you want to drift down to Natchez?"

Tom stuck down the iron point of the pole, and his surprise was great when he felt mud bottom ten feet below the surface, for the river looked like some vast inland sea. Alternately he and Andy went to the bow of the keelboat, planted their poles, and pushed their way back to the stern, walking the foot-wide plank outside the gunwale. And as they worked, the *Phoebe Ann* nosed up against the sluggish current and started for the Missouri.

It was a heart-breaking task for untrained muscles. An hour of it was all that either of the lads could stand at first. Ezra Lockwood and Brad Bunker bent their stalwart backs to the poles and relieved the boys after a little. Instead of the five and six and seven miles an hour that they had logged as they drifted down the Ohio, the travelers found themselves fortunate if they gained more than a mile an hour against the slow current of the larger river.

But by night they had learned the trick of poling. No sudden shoves, but a steady, even lean against the end of the pole, a slow, firm step on the walking plank, and a twist of the wrist at the end of each stroke, to free the point from the mud—that was the secret of it.

They held their course close in by the Illinois shore and stopped, when evening fell, a scant ten miles above the Ohio mouth. It was a wild, strange country that they had entered, now. The Mississippi seemed to have a life of its own, unlike the familiar wilderness of woods and mountains to which the Lockwoods were accustomed. Low bluffs and desolate swamps bordered the river, and as they made their boat fast in the edge of the reeds, thousands of ducks, geese and other waterfowl rose with a great uproar of wings and voices. The light was still good enough for Tom's uncle to bring down a brace of fine geese,

which Cub, now his old self once more, retrieved from the swamp and brought aboard. With this welcome addition to their fare, the travelers had a merry supper and went to bed feeling that the final stage of their journey was well begun.

The days that followed were far from comfortable, for the early summer heat had settled over the river, and the sun beat down without mercy on the heads of the *Phoebe Ann's* toiling crew. The mosquitoes, too, began to make their presence felt. At night the voyagers had to use the netting which Ezra Lockwood had been wise enough to bring from Philadelphia.

Andy, who had never seen anything of the sort, scoffed at the suggestion that he should drape a square of it over his bed on the deck. "A real hunter an' riverman don't hev sech tender skin!" he snorted. But after a night or two of restless slapping, he gave in.

On the fifth day after entering the Mississippi, they worked up around a huge bend in the river which took them eastward for several miles, before it swung to the northwest again. Tom and Andy happened to be resting, amidships, when the channel took its mighty turn.

"Le's see," said Andy, "how long's it been since we left the cave in the rocks—more'n a week, ain't it?"

"Today's the eighth day," Tom replied.

"Eight days—wal, that ain't so bad. An' yet here's one place where a feller could make a heap sight better time by land. We've come right close to two hunderd mile, on the rivers, but from that bend straight acrost to Jericho's cave is only about a hunderd an' ten. That's a three-day trip, hossback—mebbe six days, afoot, ef ye knew the trails."

At that moment Ezra Lockwood called the two boys to take their shift at the poles. But Tom had cause to ponder further on Andy's words a half hour later, as he plodded up and down the starboard walking plank. It was late afternoon, and while a riotous sunset of tumbled golden clouds lit the western sky, the Illinois bluffs, a quarter of a mile away, were bathed in a clear, pale light that made every bush and tree stand out distinctly.

Chancing to glance toward the bluff, Tom saw something moving across a little break in the trees near the top. He watched, not sure at first what sort of creature it might be. Then, as the trees thinned still more, he saw that it was a man, walking with a quick, jerky motion, as if the ground were uneven. Or was he limping? Before the boy could answer that question the figure had disappeared, diving suddenly into the brush.

Tom said nothing to his uncle or Andy about the strange apparition. He had no wish to alarm them when there was such a slight foundation for his uneasiness. In the back of his mind lurked the feeling that there was some connection between this skulker on the bluffs and the two shots they had heard, just after leaving the cave.

Since the poling had begun, Ezra Lockwood had discontinued the regular watch at night, feeling that all hands were too tired after the heavy work of the day. But that evening, when they moored the keelboat on the eastern shore, Tom quietly primed his rifle and prepared for a lonely vigil. Until after midnight he kept himself awake; then his weary head drooped and he dozed, fitfully. Some slight noise—he could not tell what it was—woke him suddenly. It was pitch dark, and he sat perfectly still, his rifle across his knees, listening. A deep growl came from Cub, close by Tom's elbow. Then, after a long moment of waiting, they heard, very faintly, the snap of a trodden stick, many yards away, up the shore. Cub, quivering with eagerness, would have dashed after the marauder at once if his owner had not held him tightly by the collar.

After a while Tom tied the dog to a deck ring and dropped off once more into a troubled slumber. But this time he was undisturbed till morning.

CHAPTER XXIII

ST. LOUIS, in that spring of 1805, was as interesting a place for two boys to wander about in as any town on the American continent. Originally it had been a French trading post, built by the old voyageurs, and the language which Tom and Andy heard most, as they walked up and down the pleasant lanes and rickety wharves, was the language of old France. Andy had a smattering of the tongue from his life on the river, and Tom had picked up a phrase or two from the French refugees who had come to Pennsylvania following the Revolution. Between them, they managed to talk to chattering mademoiselles and gruff-voiced trappers alike, and they acquired a deal of information about the things they saw.

Besides the French people there were a few families of Spaniards, relics of the days when St. Louis was the Spanish capital of the whole upper valley. And everywhere, almost as numerous as the French, were the Americans—keen-faced Yankees, smiling Kentuckians, sturdy fellows from Virginia and Pennsylvania and New York State.

There had been thousands of settlers from the Eastern seaboard in the Mississippi Valley even before the Louisiana Purchase. And when, two years earlier, Thomas Jefferson had bought that tremendous tract of land from Napoleon, thousands more had pushed westward, following the flag.

Tom and Andy stood proudly, with bared heads, as they watched that banner snapping bravely from the staff above the old fort. It was the same fort from which William Clark and Meriwether Lewis had set out on their momentous expedition into the unexplored Northwest, and though they had not yet returned, strange stories of their deeds and discoveries, relayed back by natives, trappers and fur traders, were told in awed whispers in the taverns.

A tall schooner or two from the New England ports lay at the wharves, along with scores of flatboats, keelboats, French bateaux and pirogues, skiffs and canoes.

In the midst of this motley fleet, six days after leaving the great bend, Ezra Lockwood moored the *Phoebe Ann*. Provisions were needed before the travelers went farther, and as St. Louis was the last real outpost of civilization, it was necessary for them to lay in a supply of such commodities as powder and lead.

It happened that the merchants were nearly out of powder when the party landed, but as a cargo of it was expected daily from New Orleans, Ezra Lockwood resolved to wait. And thus it was that the two boys had several days of leisure in which to look around the town.

Most of the first two days ashore were spent in carrying aboard the boat such provisions as were available, and in answering letters.

Everyone in the Lockwood party except Andy had found some mail waiting in St. Louis. Some of the letters had left Philadelphia by sailing packet a full month after the travelers had departed and had reached the town in advance of them. One message in particular had an interest for every one. It was from Charles Coleman, up the Missouri, urging them to "start from Philadelphia at once, whether by wagon or sailing vessel." The first year's crop had been remarkably abundant, he said, and they were preparing an extra piece of ground for the Lockwoods to plant.

One word of warning he gave them, namely to be "on guard against the rascally fellows led by one Wilson, who rob and murder travelers both above and below the Falls of the Ohio."

Once on the Mississippi, he went on to say, all danger would be over. The settlers and fur traders were friendly, as were the natives they'd encounter east of the Kansas River.

Tom's uncle and aunt were elated over this report, and Andy confirmed it by saying that he had never heard of river pirates up the Missouri. Tom kept his own counsel, and fervently hoped that they had seen the last of one particular outlaw.

On the fifth day of their stay, the expected schooner from downriver dropped anchor off the town, and by midafternoon Ezra Lockwood had been able to fill his lockers with powder. The *Phoebe Ann* was ready to sail, once more.

That night Tom and Andy went ashore, strolling up along the riverfront in the half-light of the spring evening. There was bustle and excitement in the little shops and taverns, for two Shawnee in a canoe had brought the news that the fur fleet had passed the Platte.

The fur fleet! In a few days a hundred boats would land and a thousand boatmen and trappers would be swarming along the shore and the streets. Tons of pelts would fill the warehouses— skins of beaver, mink and otter, fox and wolf and bear taken through the snowy months and brought down to be marketed now that the grip of the winter ice was broken in the Northern rivers.

The coming of the fur boats was the great event of the year in old St. Louis, and the boys were half sorry they were not to stay and see the fun.

"Buckeye Ben and Ba'r Hanson'll probably be along in a few days, too," said Tom. "I'd like to see Buckeye Ben try a round of shooting with some of these Missouri trappers that the folks here brag about. I reckon he'd—what do you see— what is it, Andy?"

They had come to a rather high part of the bank, at the upper end of the town, when Andy, stopping suddenly, had crouched to peer downward through the bushes that screened them from the river.

Tom's voice dropped to a whisper as he saw his friend's hand raised in warning, and he crept forward till he, too, could see what lay below. Not twenty feet down, tied to a stump and lying close in to the shore under overhanging branches, was a French pirogue—a long craft and slender, with a stub of a mast for sailing, and a black and white tarpaulin stretched on poles for a shelter astern. A pierced tin lantern hung on one of these supports, and cast a dim, diffused light over the two men who sprawled amidships. One—he was facing toward the boys—was a Spaniard, with a dark, cruel hawk's face. He had a dirty orange handkerchief knotted about his head. A stubble of black beard and huge brass earrings completed his villainous appearance. He was talking low and earnestly to the other man, who sat with his back to the shore. The rays of the lantern that fell on him were few and uncertain, but Tom made out a frayed blue jacket, draping gaunt shoulders that were hunched familiarly; and a felt hat, pulled so far down to the left that its brim almost brushed the fellow's neck.

The boys were kneeling there in the edge of the bushes, barely breathing in the excitement of their discovery, when a tramp of feet became audible, close by. Four or five figures loomed in the deepening dusk. A husky voice muttered, "Here, this is the place," and the new arrivals plunged into the brush, a few yards away, and went scrambling down to the river's edge. One by one they went aboard the moored pirogue, nodding silently to the Spaniard and his companion. An ugly looking lot of men they were, as they lounged on the thwarts—wharf rats and riverfront loafers, all of them, by their appearance.

"All right," rasped a voice that made Tom and Andy jump with its harsh suddenness, "let's get out away from shore an' talk things over."

The man in the blue coat got to his feet as he spoke, and turned toward the lantern the scarred, leathery face of Earless Jake Rogers.

Two of the other men picked up poles, and as the mooring rope was loosed, the pirogue shot out from shore, vanishing in the dusk that veiled the river.

The boys lost no time in getting back to the *Phoebe Ann* and recounting what they had seen. There was a grave look on Ezra Lockwood's face as he heard them. "Now that this fellow has escaped," he said, "there's no telling what mischief he may be planning. Almost certainly he has seen some of us, or recognized the boat, and he knows, of course, that Andy's chest is aboard here. What would you say, Andy, lad, to leaving the money with Major Morton, at the fort, for safe keeping? There are no banks in the town, but I think the Major would take it for us."

Andy readily agreed to this arrangement, and immediately after breakfast the next morning the chest was slung on two poles and carried ashore. It took the four of them—Tom, Andy, Tom's uncle and Brad Bunker—to bear the massive box through the streets, but when they arrived at the fort they found Major Morton's welcome quite as cordial as Ezra Lockwood had anticipated. The officer had the chest placed in his own strongroom, and on hearing that one of the Muskingum men's outlaw prisoners was at large, he at once sent a detail of soldiers to search the waterfront. Meanwhile the visitors were treated to an excellent luncheon, and though no trace of Rogers had been found when the soldiers returned, they all left the fort in high spirits.

"What do you say to making our start now?" the elder Lockwood asked, as they boarded the keelboat again. "The whole afternoon's ahead of us, and we can be up into the muddy water before we camp."

There were few preparations to make. The mooring rope was coiled aboard, Tom and Brad Bunker took the poles, and with a farewell wave to St. Louis, the crew of the *Phoebe Ann* started on once more.

CHAPTER XXIV

EZRA LOCKWOOD had been right in his forecast. Before dark had fallen, the keelboat, nosing up the west bank, had entered a broad belt of yellow water that reached half way across the river. The Missouri was near at hand.

A thick pall of river mist settled over everything after sunset, and they slept aboard the boat that night. Brad Bunker, who had kept his farmhand habits, rose with the sun and routed out Andy. When Tom awoke it was to find the *Phoebe Ann* already a mile or more above last night's anchorage, and plowing northward with the steady impetus of the poles. As soon as he had washed he took Andy's place while the redhaired lad ate breakfast, and so they carried on through the morning, taking turns on the walking planks.

The scenery along the banks that they passed so slowly now was beginning to change. Here and there between the clumps of woods, the prairie could be seen stretching away for miles, a gently rolling sea of grass.

Just at noon they began bearing to the left around an enormous bend, where the boys, looking off to the right, could see the Mississippi coming down from the North, while westward, in the direction they were moving, stretched the broad face of the Missouri. They had come to the joining place of the two mightiest rivers of the continent.

Up the Missouri, thick and yellow with the silt of a thousand spring freshets, the keelboat moved, a dozen miles a day.

Sometimes, for hours, they worked their way along at a snail's pace, feeling with their poles for deeper water off one of the treacherous sand bars that blocked the channel. Once or twice they found themselves aground on a bar before they could change their course, and had to labor doggedly to dig and shove their way off.

The weather held fair and the sun beat down fiercely on the yellow river, between its high yellow banks. There were no settlements—not even a hunter's cabin along the shore. Through the fringe of trees that crowned the bluff, the travelers caught occasional glimpses of flat, hot plains, breaking the woods to the northward. It was a totally different sort of country from the wilderness of forest that they had traversed as they floated down the Ohio. But both Tom and Andy felt themselves drawn to this new land, with its rolling distances.

On the sixth day after leaving St. Louis, Andy was just finishing a two-hour shift with the poles when he suddenly hailed Tom, at the other end of the boat.

"Look over there, just to the west'ard o' that clump o' cottonwoods," he called. "Do you see somethin' movin'?"

Tom shaded his eyes and gazed intently in the direction where Andy was pointing. "Yes," said he. "Men on horseback—quite a bunch of them, I should say!"

Andy shook his sorrel-thatched head. "That ain't my guess," he said. "I never seen buffalo, but—"

"You're right," cried Tom, excitedly. "That's what they are! Get your rifle and come on ashore in the canoe. We can catch up with the boat before it's our turn to pole again."

"Good 'nough," agreed Andy. "Only don't give me a rifle. From what I hear, I want that big ol' smoothbore gun o' your uncle's, an' some solid ounce ball."

"Suit yourself," said Tom. "I'll stick to my long-barreled

rifle, with a good heavy charge in her. I've seen her kill buck and bear, so I'm not a mite worried about those fellows."

"Huh! Buck an' bear!" snorted Andy. "Wait till you git close to a buffalo an' you'll be too scairt to shoot!"

They left Cub behind, for they did not know how he would act in the presence of this kind of game. As soon as the canoe was beached, both lads scrambled up a ravine to the top of the bluff and looked eagerly off to the north.

The herd was still in sight, a scattered group of tiny dark spots, crawling slowly westward on the face of the great plain. Now and then, as the boys hurried forward, a rise in the ground would offer them partial concealment, but for the most part they merely stooped a little as they ran, trusting to the near-sightedness of the animals to keep them from being seen. The wind, what there was of it, blew over from the southwest, favoring them rather than the game.

The leaders of the procession vanished, slow moving, behind a low hill, and as the rest of the buffalo went trooping after them, out of sight, Tom straightened up and began to increase his speed.

"Now's our chance, Andy," he gasped. "Keep the hill between them and us, and we can get right up on top of 'em!"

Together they crossed the quarter mile that intervened, racing through the knee-high grass. The hill which concealed the herd was little more than a mound, rising a scant twenty feet above the prairie. Up its side the boys crawled breathlessly, and paused just below the crest to cock their guns. Then they thrust their heads cautiously up through the grass. Tom's first glimpse was disappointing. It showed him the plain, a hundred yards away—empty! He hitched himself an inch or two higher and suddenly his hair seemed to stand on end. For there, not ten paces below him, were the biggest animals he had ever seen—huge, shaggy, ponderous creatures that munched at the grass, grunting and snorting, and rolled their eyes, set deep under their enormous, hairy foreheads.

"Great holy jumpin' 'hosaphats!" he heard Andy whisper beside him, and then, he hardly knew how, he was aiming a very unsteady rifle at the nearest bull. Once—he had no idea where or when—he had heard that the place to shoot a buffalo was through the heart and lungs. Leisurely the great brute he had selected moved forward his left foreleg, and *"Crack!— bang!"* the two guns spoke together. The bull broke into a lumbering gallop that took him a score of yards before he stumbled, rolled half over, got up and fell again. Around him the rest of the herd—twenty or thirty young bulls—scattered in all directions, tails aloft and beards sweeping the earth. In a moment the hurrying thunder of their hoofs had died away and only a cloud of yellow dust remained.

The boys scrambled to their feet and went toward their quarry, a little shakily. By the time they reached the bull he was quite dead. Andy dropped on his knees beside the enormous body and examined the wound back of the beast's left shoulder.

"There y'are!" he cried triumphantly, "there's smooth bore an' ounce ball fer ye!" Tom stooped beside him. "All right," he answered, "but there's the hole from my bullet, right above. We'll divide the honors, Andy. Probably neither one would have stopped him, alone."

Their attempts at skinning the gigantic animal were rather clumsy, at first. However, they brought all their hunting experience into play, and soon a good part of the carcass was laid bare. As much meat as they could carry was out from the tender portions of the hump and loins, and the boys set out for the river, leaving the rest of the body to the wolves, which were already skulking in the nearby grass.

"How do you suppose buffalo ever got this far east?" asked

Tom. "I thought the big herds weren't seen much this side of the Platte."

"Reckon they roam 'round to suit theirselves, wherever ther's forage," Andy replied. "I've hearn tell of 'em over in Illinois, even. This was jest a small herd o' bulls. The cows with their calves stay nearer to home, I've heard the hunters say, but the bulls go off in leetle bunches wherever the grass is good. Anyhow, we got our first one, an', boy, didn't he look big, when we crep' over the top?"

"Big as a church," said Tom. "It's really too bad to kill one of 'em, when you can't carry away a tenth part of the meat. It seems like a mean trick, and a waste, besides."

"Pshaw!" Andy snorted. "They's millions of 'em. 'Sides we needed fresh meat, so we had a good excuse. Next time, though, let's don't waste lead both shootin' at the same bull. Do you reckon we'll keep on a-findin' 'em all the way up the Missouri? Say, what in the—look here, Tom—look at this!"

They had reached the riverbank once more, and Andy, as he spoke, was bending low over the yellow mud beside the dugout. Tom, peering with him, beheld freshly trampled boot-tracks—not his own soft moccasin marks, nor Andy's, but the dent of hobnailed heels. The canoe lay as they had left it, except that the forward paddle lay in the bottom with its blade pointing toward the bow. Andy called Tom's attention to it.

"I never drop a paddle that-a-way. Neither do you. I allus leave the handle end p'inted forrard, whar I kin reach it. These fellers must ha' looked the boat over pretty careful, an' decided they didn't want it."

"Where did they come from?" said Tom. "Probably from the river. Yes, here's another track over here, and I reckon that's where they pulled their own boat up." He pointed to a shallow indentation in the sand at the edge of the water. It had been washed away to such an extent that the shape of the prow that made it could not even be guessed.

"Wal, whoever 'twas," Andy concluded, "they've gone 'long 'bout their business. Reckon mebbe they was trappers from the fur fleet."

"Not in hobnailed boots," Tom replied. "But I don't know who else it might be, except—well, let's be getting along."

They stowed their guns and the packs of buffalo meat in the canoe and shoved off with pole and paddle.

CHAPTER XXV

THERE WERE WIDE EDDIES and stretches of slack water along
the north bank at the point where Tom and Andy launched
their dugout, after the buffalo hunt. By taking advantage of
these currents they made excellent speed for the first half mile.
After that the work became harder, though they were still able
to move upstream much faster than the *Phoebe Ann*. Ahead of
them, perhaps a mile away, a sandy point and a series of small
islands and bars jutted out nearly to the middle of the river, and
it was evident that the keelboat had rounded this point, for she
was nowhere in sight. There was, however, a black object far
over toward the south bank and some distance ahead, which
Tom pronounced either a vessel of some kind or one of the
huge logs which were often encountered on the river.

It was in fact a boat, as they soon determined. Drawing
gradually abreast of it, they could see the long, sharp lines of a
French pirogue, poling lazily up against the current.

"I don't like the looks of that craft, Andy," said Tom. "She's
too much like the one we saw that night in St. Louis. Let's dig
in! The *Phoebe Ann* must be just around that point."

They plied the pole and paddle steadily and were soon past
the pirogue, which seemed to have come somewhat nearer the
northern shore. But Andy, glancing over his shoulder a moment
later, gave a shout of dismay. The larger vessel had hoisted a
square, brown sail, and with the wind abeam, and the poles
flashing rapidly along her sides, she was drawing up on the
dugout at a furious rate.

The riverboy braced his feet more firmly and fairly lifted the canoe forward with the pole.

"Tom," he shouted, "that boat's got a black and white tarpaulin astern. It's Rogers, right enough, an' he's a-pullin' up on us fast!"

Tom did not waste time in looking back. Ahead of them, but still nearly half a mile away, he saw a narrow gap of water, between the point and the landward end of one of the sandy islets. And for this slender channel he steered, driving his paddle with might and main.

The smacking report of a rifle reached their ears almost at that moment, and a bullet went skipping past along the water.

"Never mind those," cried Tom. "They aren't within range yet!"

Apparently he was right. During the next breathless minute or two, scattering shots from the pirogue fell short or ricocheted harmlessly by. But then came a solid, jarring *plunk* that told the boys their canoe must have been hit. Tom, watching the bottom anxiously for signs of a leak, decided that the bullet must have buried itself in the thick wood of the stern. Another shot, a moment later, ripped a long splinter from one gunwale, and a third sang dangerously close to Andy's head.

With a rush they entered the narrow channel between the point and the bar. Swirling water was around them, and the banks drew very close on either side. Tom's paddle touched bottom. In two more strokes he felt the canoe scraping the mud, and in three they were hard aground. "Stay where you are, and pole!" he shouted to Andy, and scrambling out, he pushed the dugout forward with all his strength. The grip of the mud yielded gradually and the craft slid forward, then floated clear on the other side. Tom jumped to his place in the stern with a final mighty shove.

The right-hand bank curved sharply northward just beyond, and the boys were soon out of sight of their pursuers.

They were safe for the moment at least. Because of her deeper draft, the pirogue was unable to take the shortcut across the bar which the canoe had just negotiated. She must travel nearly half a mile to clear the outer end of the sandy island, and before Earless Jake could get within gunshot again, the boys knew that they could reach the *Phoebe Ann,* now visible beyond a bend in the shore, a short distance ahead.

The keelboat's square sail was spread to the quartering breeze, and with Brad Bunker poling on the lee side, she was moving at a reasonably rapid rate of speed. Ezra Lockwood hailed them anxiously from the afterdeck as they drew near.

"What was that firing, just now?" he asked. "We were afraid of the natives."

Tom and Andy came alongside and passed their guns and the buffalo meat into the waist of the larger craft. They were still panting from their dash up the river when they climbed aboard.

"Natives!" said Tom. "No, Uncle Ezra. That was Jake Rogers' crew, and they'll be after us again in five minutes. Here comes the boat around the point now."

The Pennsylvania gunsmith was a man of ready action in an emergency. He gave his orders sharp and quick.

"Brad, leave the poling and come take the tiller. There's enough wind to keep steerage way on her. Tom and Andy, take your rifles, and the two spare ones in the locker and get them loaded. Lay out bullets, powder and wadding where they'll be handy. Then make yourselves snug back of the gunwales and let them have it good and hot as soon as they begin firing at us."

So saying, he took his own gun and settled himself behind the corner of the cabin. Tom went aft to the sternpost, and Andy took up a position amidships. They did not have long to wait, for the pirogue was clipping toward them through the water with all the speed her polers could give her.

When she was about three hundred yards distant, a puff of smoke came from her bows, followed by a report, and the *plop* of a spent bullet.

Tom heard a chuckle from Andy. "I was wishin', back there'n the canoe, that we hed time to spit a leetle lead back at those polecats," said the riverboy, grimly. "Now it sure looks like we're goin' to git our chance."

Another shot and then another sang past them, as the pirogue drew closer. "All ready," said the elder Lockwood, quietly. "Give it to them!"

Almost in the same second, three bullets sped from the *Phoebe Ann*. One struck the smaller boat's hull right at the water line, with a spurt of spray. Another tore a crude hole in the lower part of the sail. And the third—Tom's—went raking the length of the vessel just above the gunwale with deadly effect. The wind brought to their ears an anguished yell from someone aboard the pirogue, and suddenly, before another volley could be discharged, the helmsman of Rogers' craft swung her sharply to the left, edging out of range.

The keelboat's marksmen fired two or three more shots, "jes' to show 'em we got plenty o' powder," as Andy expressed it. Then they turned energetically to the poling once more.

"Let's make what speed we can," said Ezra Lockwood. "For the present, those varmints have had all they want of us. They'll hardly try another attack in daylight, and before night we may reach some camp or settlement."

They pushed on steadily, hour after hour, holding as close to the north bank as snags and sandbars would permit. Less than a mile ahead of them, when the river ran straight, they could catch occasional glimpses of the pirogue. The wind died out as sunset approached, and either because of this or because the outlaw crew wished to keep the keelboat in sight, the smaller craft did not increase its lead.

Daylight faded at length, and dusk began to shadow the river. Ezra Lockwood frowned as he scanned the shore. "There seems to be nothing for it but to tie up for the night," he said. "But at least we can throw an anchor out on one side and moor to a tree on the other, so as to be a little way from the bank."

They steered inshore and Tom dropped the clumsy mud-hook over the bow. As he did so he saw the pirogue, far upstream, likewise swinging in toward the right-hand bank. The anchor by itself failed to hold the *Phoebe Ann* against the steady downrush of the current, but before it had dragged far, Tom and Andy got quickly into the canoe and carried a mooring line ashore. Once this rope was fastened around a tree trunk, it took up most of the boat's pull, and the anchor, relieved of part of its strain, caught in the mud and held the craft firmly in place, half a dozen yards from shore.

"We'll stand regular watches, now," said the leader of the party, as they prepared to eat supper, "and with this water between us and the bank, they can hardly take us by surprise."

"No," Tom answered, "but we make it easier for them to surprise us if we just sit here and wait. I think we should try to beat them at their own game. "Why can't Andy and I start up along shore in the canoe after a while, and find out what they plan to do? They'll never see us, in the dark."

"Yes, siree!" Andy broke in. "We've got to be almighty foxy with that crowd or they'll start playin' the fox with us. Jake Rogers ain't goin' to spend the night sleepin'—not Earless Jake! An' the only way for us to know what he's up to is to watch him. He's a skunk, right enough, but he don't leave no scent."

Ezra Lockwood considered a moment or two, then nodded at Tom. "Go," he said. "We can manage here well enough, in case of trouble. Brad and I will both keep watch until you come back. But be cautious. Don't show yourselves for an instant, whatever happens."

There was a young moon setting in the west when the boys began their preparations for departure, but by the time they climbed into the dugout, pitchy darkness had settled over the river. Hunting knives and rifles were all they carried. Cub, much to his own disgust, was left to help guard the *Phoebe Ann.*

They hugged the looming shadow of the north bank, and stole along up the stream, paddling silently, never taking their blades from the water. The woods came down densely, almost to the river's edge, and there was something sinister in the way the wind moaned in the treetops. The boys had advanced half a mile or more when a faint sound came to them from up the bank to their right. As they both paused to listen, it was repeated —the sharp, unmistakable crack of a trampled stick. Then the wind came with a soft whoosh overhead, and carried away all the smaller noises of the forest. The only sound that reached the boys, as they crouched there in the canoe, was the muffled howl of a wolf, somewhere on the prairie to the southward.

Tom restrained an impulse to ask Andy if he had heard. Instead, he drove the canoe forward silently, with a deep, slow stroke, and waited with all his senses keyed to the highest pitch. The noise, whatever had caused it, was not repeated.

They were close to the outlaws' landing place, now—so close that the low, red light of the dying fire flickered through the trees. Without a word, Tom guided their craft into the shore and they stepped out on a narrow stretch of sand, beaching the dugout with as little noise as possible. Then, taking up their rifles, they crawled up the bank in the direction of the fire.

The glow of the embers dimly lighted a level, open space at the edge of the low bluff. There were remnants of a meal, and a dirty skillet or two strewn about the place, and at the farther side of the circle of light were two men. One—a great hulk of a fellow with a bandage around his head—lay on a buffalo robe, tossing and cursing restlessly. Beside him sat a stony-faced native, who seemed to doze, careless of the groans of his companion.

Tom and Andy watched the pair for a moment, then wriggled noiselessly back, down the bank.

"Let's take a look at their boat," Andy whispered, and led the way cautiously forward, keeping below the crest of the bluff. They could see the pirogue, a vague dark splotch in the starlight, and the black line of a rope, running taut to a tree stump, above. Nearer they crept, stopping to listen and look every moment or two. At length they were so close that they could see every inch of the boat—even the planking beneath the striped tarpaulin astern. There was no one aboard.

Tom saw Andy draw his skinning knife and whet the blade once or twice on his moccasin sole. Then the riverboy climbed upward till he could lay a hand on the mooring line. As he did so, his foot dislodged a bit of gravel that skipped downward with a tiny rattling sound. The boys waited breathlessly but all was silent. Andy drew the keen edge of his knife across the rope four or five times, and the severed ends dropped apart. Tom, waiting below, gave the pirogue a strong push, so that it swung out, revolving slowly, into the current. And in that second, a sudden, smothered cry burst from Andy. Tom whirled in time to see the riverlad rolling down the bank, locked in a fierce grapple with the native they had seen beside the campfire. The man was far bigger than Andy and his weight told, as the struggling pair slid downward. He pinned the boy beneath him and flung aloft a naked arm, in the fist of which a big knife gleamed.

There was no time to choose weapons. Tom was only a stride away and he had his rifle muzzle in his hands. As he sprang in he swung it up like a club.

The man's arm had already started to descend when the gunstock crashed upon his skull, and the knife dropped from his fingers as he slumped backward into the sand. A noise came from the bank, above, and the voice of the wounded man could be heard, calling querulously.

"Quick, Andy," Tom whispered, "are you hurt?"

"Not much—let's get out of this," the riverboy replied, and he started, limping a little, in the direction of the canoe. Tom caught him by the arm, helping him forward. "It's my ankle," said Andy. "I turned it jest a mite, when that devil jumped me."

They got into the dugout and Tom took up his paddle, while Andy sat in the bottom and wound a handkerchief tightly about his wrenched ankle. The night was unusually dark. Twenty yards from shore they could barely see the outlines of trees on the bank. The drifting pirogue had long since vanished in the blurry blackness that hung over the river.

Tom steered the canoe dexterously among the swirling eddies, and the current bore them rapidly nearer to the *Phoebe Ann's* landing place. Andy suddenly leaned forward. "Listen," said he, "that's ol' Cub a-yelpin'. What do ye s'pose he's treed now?"

Tom poised his paddle for a second and caught the sound of the terrier's barks in a furious staccato. "Something's wrong down there," he said. "I shouldn't wonder if that's where we'll find Jake and the rest of his gang. We'd better hustle."

As if to corroborate his words a rifle shot rang out sharply below. Another followed, then four or five at once. A scattered report or two came to their ears and all was still once more, except for Cub's fierce barking. Andy crawled forward and knelt in the bow of the dugout. As his paddle began to dip in unison with Tom's they shot down the stream at racehorse speed.

The silence was ominous as they drew close to the landing place. Even the terrier was momentarily quiet. Tom's eyes strained into the dark, searching for the black bulk of the *Phoebe Ann*. He steered inshore, expecting, at each stroke, to see the side of the keelboat loom above him. All of a sudden there was a splash in the water close to the canoe, and Cub thrust his nose over the gunwale, whining and scratching frantically with his paws. Tom started to lift him in, but at that instant a hard voice spoke from the bank, a dozen feet away. "Surrender!" it ordered sharply. "Put down them paddles, or I'll blow ye into the middle o' next week!"

Before either of the boys could make a motion to escape, the bow of the canoe grated on the shore, and several pairs of rough hands hauled her high on the beach.

CHAPTER XXVI

"Give us a light, there!"

Tom, standing erect beside the canoe, with a pistol muzzle pressed uncomfortably hard against his chest, saw a glow of tinder follow the command, and waited for the lantern to be lit. His mind was working coolly. Already he had a fair idea of what had happened, and was casting about for some means of escape. Evidently the *Phoebe Ann* had been attacked, and his uncle had been forced to cut the moorings. The boys, arriving just after the keelboat's departure, had run into the very arms of the outlaw crew, who, from the darkness of the shore, had been able to see the canoe on the water without being seen.

As the tallow dip in the lantern flared, Tom saw Jake Rogers limping towards him, his leathery face wrinkled in a sneering grin. Five other sinister, armed figures stood in a close ring. One, the wicked-looking Spaniard in the orange headcloth, held a great buffalo pistol against the front of Tom's hunting shirt and two or three paces away another riverman had Andy covered with a rifle. In the brush, just outside the circle of light, Cub growled unceasingly.

So for a moment they all remained. Then Rogers' gloating smile changed to a scowl of malice, and his harsh voice snapped out a command.

"Rope 'em up an' let's get movin'!" he ordered.

One of the gang pulled a hatchet from his belt and cut down a three-inch birch sapling which he speedily trimmed into a pole a dozen feet in length. To the middle of this pole the outlaws proceeded to tie the two boys, one on either side, binding their wrists fast behind their backs and hauling them tight with a bend around the sapling. Then one man picked up the boys' rifles with the knives which had been taken from them, two others seized the ends of the pole, and the party set out westward along the bank. Tom and Andy, stumbling forward, with the rope chafing painfully at their wrists, had little opportunity to talk to each other. A cold anger filled the Pennsylvania boy. He knew the hatred that Earless Jake bore him, and guessed that terrible things might lie ahead, up the shore. Yet he felt no fear—only a fierce desire to come to grips with his enemy. If only he could loose his hands—

The lantern bearer was in front, leading the way, and Tom knew that in the darkness the rear guard could not see the bonds that held him to the pole. He had thick, strong wrists— almost as thick as his hands. With a gradual, steady movement, he began pushing and tugging his arms up and down in opposite directions, loosening, a strand at a time, the four thicknesses of rope lashed about his wrists. It was a slow process for it had to be done without arousing the suspicions of the men behind. At last Tom worked his right hand free. Leaving his own left wrist still half tied, he began on the knots that bound Andy. However he had to work awkwardly, behind his back, and his straining fingers seemed to make no progress.

They had been pushing forward during this time over the roughest sort of footing, following what seemed to be an old deer trail through the brush. And now, all too soon, they were filing out into the open space on the bluff where the campfire still smoldered. Tom gave up his efforts to loose Andy, and making sure that he could pull free in an instant if necessary, he took a turn with the rope about his own wrists, holding it in place as if he were still tied.

The man with the bandaged head sat up, swaying weakly as they approached, and said something in a hoarse voice to Rogers, who was leading the way.

Earless Jake turned sharply and looked toward the bank. "What's that!" he said, and then shouted, "Louis! Ho, Louis!" There was no answer, and as Rogers started at his quick, jerky gait for the edge of the bluff, Tom felt Andy's muscles grow taut, beside him.

The leader of the rivermen disappeared for only a moment or two. When he climbed up the bank once more, into the light of the now rekindled fire, his face was dark with passion. A low, continuous stream of oaths came from between his clenched teeth as he limped nearer. He came and stood before the boys, looking at them with eyes that were narrowed to mere slits.

"Wal, ye dirty young whelps," he cried, his voice breaking into a kind of snarl, "what's goin' to happen now ye've brung on yerselves. Two o' my pals laid out, an' now ye've cut our boat adrift. That's a matter fer shootin', on the Missoura. Only you ain't goin' to be shot—neither one of ye. Remember, I ain't no Jericho Wilson—softhearted, like."

An insane glitter came into the man's eyes. "I asked Jericho fer you, onct," he pointed a quivering finger at Tom. "I asked him, an' if he'd let me do with ye like I wanted, the big swine would ha' been alive today. This time I'm a-goin' to make sure of ye. We kin take keer o' gittin' yer uncle an' the money chest tomorrow."

Tom flashed an amazed glance at Andy. "The money chest!" Then the river pirates thought it was still aboard the keelboat!

Earless Jake took a stride toward the boys. "Pedro!" he yelled to the dark-faced Spaniard, "get that fire mad hot. We're gwineter smell moccasin leather burnin' round yere in a minute!"

Another riverman drew near with a length of rawhide in his hand, and the gaunt leader beckoned to him, eagerly. "That's it, Mike!" he growled. "Tie this young devil's shanks together." The man stooped in front of Tom and began binding his feet with the thong. Rogers turned away to hurry preparations at the fire. Tom swept the clearing with a quick eye. Nobody was watching them. His right hand came from behind him, and in a single swift movement he pulled the outlaw's knife from its sheath, over the hip. So dexterously was it done that the man kept on tugging at the hide strip around his legs, ignorant of what had happened. Tom's mind was working like lightning. His first impulse was to strike and run. He could outdistance any of them, he knew. But there was Andy—fast to the pole!

Quick as thought, Tom whipped the knife behind him. His left hand found the knot at Andy's wrists, but there was no time to cut it. Already the riverman was finishing his work. Tom slipped the knife, blade, hilt and all, into the back of Andy's trousers, till it was hidden below his belt. Then, as the man straightened up, he twisted the untied rope about his hands again.

Earless Jake returned from the fire.

"Guess them logs is gittin' hot 'nough, now!" he snarled, and came around behind the boys. Instantly his eye fell on the rope and he saw that Tom had untied his hands.

"Hah!" laughed Rogers, short and ugly. "Figgered ye'd git away ag'in, eh? Wal, luck don't keep on ferever, an' yours is played out! Come here, Pedro. We'll put the wing clippers onto him."

Tom's ankles had already been bound tightly together with the greenhide thong. He was helpless to resist, so he stood quietly while Rogers and the Spaniard attached lengths of rope to each of his arms, above the elbow. He knew now what was going to happen. From Andy he had heard of the pet torture of the river pirates—the cruel, terrible "crowhop." He looked at his friend, and the firelight showed him Andy's face, white and sick beneath the freckles.

Rogers inspected the rope that bound Andy's hands. "This young turkey can't git fur, tied to that log," he said. "We'll let him watch the fun fer a while."

Then he picked up the end of the six-foot rope that hung from Tom's left arm. Pedro, the Spaniard, had hold of the other cord. Grinning they each gave a sudden jerk forward.

"Now, *hop!*" cried Earless Jake, with the voice of a fiend.

Andy saw Tom pulled almost to the ground again and again, as the poor lad tried desperately to keep his balance. All of the rivermen gathered close to the fire, laughing uproariously at the sight, and the young Kentuckian, unobserved, worked one hand inside his belt at the back, feeling for the handle of the knife Tom had hidden there. He touched the smooth leather hilt and got a purchase on it with two fingers, toiling feverishly to pull it out.

At the fire, Tom had been hauled to a point a foot or so from the edge of the flames. Two or three men took hold of each rope, now, and ranged themselves on opposite sides of the fire.

"Jump!" screamed Rogers' voice, and Tom, leaping gallantly, cleared the blazing logs by inches. Evidently they meant to play with him a little, before the frightful end.

Andy got the knife free at last. He turned it in his hand so that its edge was against the cord that bound him, and began cutting. He hardly dared look toward his friend. Every moment he expected to see him jerked back into the fire. They were forcing him to jump faster and faster, yelling hoarsely at him each time he went over the flames in his dance of death. Andy's knife blade severed two of the three turns of rope and he pulled the third one loose with a great wrench of his arms. The knife he thrust through his belt, and the birch pole he took in both hands, and started toward the fire.

He did not need to go quietly. The demonic whoops of the torturers drowned out the sound of his running feet. Twice now they had pulled Tom down at the height of his spring, so that his moccasined feet had trodden red embers at the edge of the flame. Only desperate balancing had saved him from toppling backward. The glimpse Andy caught of his face, distorted and white from pain and exhaustion, threw the redhaired boy into a sort of frenzy. He rushed at the outlaws, swinging his gigantic club wildly about his head. Before they knew it he was on them. The birch pole whistled in a twenty-foot arc and its heavy butt crashed, head high, into the nearer group of rope pullers.

They went over like nine pins. One was knocked senseless by the force of the blow, and before the other two could regain their feet, Andy had reached Tom's side. He jerked the knife from his belt and put it in the taller boy's hand. "Cut loose, quick!" he said, and swung up his unwieldy weapon for another assault.

The boy was fast as a cat on his feet, and he had need to be, for now Rogers and the men who were helping him dropped the arm rope on the other side and came charging at him with murder in their faces. Andy gave ground, jumping back and back as he whirled his sapling. He could see Tom, stooping shakily to cut the rawhide thong at his ankles, and he wanted to give him time. Meanwhile the other two rivermen had picked themselves up and were running to join in the attack.

For a moment more the boy succeeded in holding them off. Then they began closing in on him from all sides, and matters began to have an ugly look, for he knew his club was too long and heavy for continued defense. One of the outlaws fired a pistol and the ball grazed him, plucking at his sleeve. Tom was up and free now, and armed with the knife he was hurrying to the rescue. Then, suddenly, as if the pistol shot had been a summons, Cub tore out of the woods and launched himself into the midst of things, leaping straight at Rogers like a fury let loose.

For a single moment the dog's fierce onslaught drew the attention of all the rivermen away from Andy. And in that moment the boy hurled his club at Earless Jake's head, then turned and sprinted toward Tom. With every ounce of strength they had left, the two boys raced across the open space and plunged into the woods on the upriver side. For a few paces the firelight glimmered faintly on the tree trunks, but soon even this was gone, and they stumbled forward in total darkness. Tom heard the sound of a fall and then a muffled groan from Andy, to his left. The shouts of the pursuers were coming close.

"Where are you—what's the trouble?" Tom whispered, and heard his chum's voice answer, "Down in this hole! Look out— don't fall in!" Cautiously feeling the ground with his foot, he discovered a little gully, two feet or so in width, and partly grown over with grass at the top. He let himself down and found Andy huddled at the bottom. "Tumbled in yere, an' turned that cussed ankle ag'in," muttered the Kentucky boy. Tom crouched beside him, his head below the level of the ground. "Quiet!" he panted. "Here they come!"

With a smashing of twigs and a thud of running feet, the leaders went by. Then a man came carrying a torch, and passed so close that a spark from his brand fell into the gully beside them. And following him they heard a limping step and a voice that cursed with every breath. Earless Jake went almost directly over them, and his foot even slipped a little at the edge of the hole, but he ran on.

Tom gripped Andy's arm. "They're all out after us—every one of them," he whispered. "There's no guard left at the fire.

I'm going back to the edge of the clearing and see what's become of Cub."

As the boy crawled up out of the gully he could hear the searchers threshing through the brush to the westward, and here and there a torch flickered among the trees. But as the pursuit seemed to be working farther away instead of coming nearer, Tom got to his feet and started back in the direction of the fire. When he reached the fringe of trees that bordered the open space he went warily, crawling forward on his hands and knees. As he had thought, the place was deserted. At first he feared that he had come in vain. Then his eye caught a slight movement on the ground between himself and the fire. It was Cub—hurt! Tom bounded to his feet and ran across the cleared space to the dog's side. Tenderly he lifted the scarred brown head of the terrier. Cub's eyes were half closed and a great red wound ran across one side of his head and neck. At Tom's touch, the dog started and trembled. Then his stumpy tail began to wag, he caressed the boy's hand with a warm, wet tongue tip.

Tom tried to set him on his feet. "Come, boy, come on!" he whispered. But Cub's right fore leg crumpled pitifully beneath him, and he was so weak that he swayed and nearly fell. As Tom took him in his arms he heard shouts in the woods to the north. With all the speed he could muster he ran toward cover at the western edge of the clearing.

Hardly had the boy safely reached the fringe of trees when he heard voices back in the open space, and turning to peer between the tree trunks he could see four of the river pirates, led by Pedro, the Spaniard, returning to the fire. Their disappointment at failing to find their victims was evidently keen for they were swearing angrily. Tom waited to see no more, but crouched and ran forward as fast as he could. At first he had difficulty in locating the ditch in which Andy was hidden. But after he had crossed it twice he resorted to walking with very short steps, fairly feeling his way along—and so found the gully by stepping squarely into it.

Tom laid the dog gently on the sand, and reached out his hands in the dark, trying to locate his chum. "Andy—where are you?" he whispered, and in a moment he heard him, off to the left, crawling nearer along the bottom of the gully.

"Look here," Tom breathed, as the riverboy reached his side. "I found Cub, but he's hurt—bad. We've got to get water for him if we're going to save him."

" 'Tain't so fur to the bank," said Andy. "I jest crawled down the ditch a ways an' I could see starlight out through the trees."

"All right," Tom answered. "You stay here and take care of Cub. I don't think he'll bark—he's too sick."

Andy took the limp body of the terrier in his lap and Tom set out on hands and knees in the direction of the river. The gully along which he crawled was a rough channel washed out by the spring rains. It shallowed and widened in places so that it afforded scarcely any concealment, but it was still dark in the woods, and the shouts of the outlaw gang sounded far away.

As Tom pushed on he could see broadening patches of sky ahead, and knew that he was nearing the edge of the trees. A score of yards more, and the gully plunged steeply downward, between high banks. The gurgle of water reached Tom's ears. Just ahead lay the wide, shimmering surface of the river.

The boy went cautiously now. Before he emerged from his trench at the edge of the water, he looked up the shore and down. The first faint graying of dawn made things more easily distinguishable now. But a rotting stump, half a dozen yards away, was all he saw. Moving as stealthily as a cat, he reached the brink of the stream, took off one of his moccasins and started to dip it into the water.

At the very instant he stooped forward, the *"Whang!"* of a rifleshot broke the stillness. The movement probably saved his life, for the bullet passed a scant inch above his bent back. Tom yanked the hunting knife out of his belt and whirled about to face a grim figure that came at him, down the bank. Even in the semidarkness he knew that it was Jake Rogers. The man moved warily but with a sort of terrible finality. In his hand gleamed the familiar long blade, and on his gaunt face was a look of stark hatred that made Tom's blood run cold.

The boy was quick and strong but he knew he lacked the skill to cope with the greatest knife fighter on all the rivers. Therefore when Rogers made his tiger-like spring, Tom dropped his own weapon and grasped with both hands at the lean outlaw's thrusting right arm. His fingers got a momentary grip as the knife drove in, and the point failed to pierce his shirt. But with a deft twist of the wrist, Earless Jake pulled free, and the edge of the blade sliced cruelly into Tom's fingers as the outlaw leaped away.

Again, like a flash, came the attack, and this time the desperate boy ducked low, lunging at his assailant's knees. He caught the impact of Rogers' rush on his shoulder and was carried over backward into the water by the headlong plunge of the riverman. For a moment Tom struggled to get clear of his antagonist and come to the surface. As he succeeded he heard Earless Jake spluttering, a few yards off, and without looking back he swam toward the shelving bank with all his might. Twice he pulled himself up on the slippery mud only to slide back. With the fear of a knife blade in his back he made a third tremendous effort, and scrambled out almost exhausted on the shore.

Right in front of him, as he gained his feet, Tom saw the knife he had dropped at Rogers' first charge. He snatched it up and turned, staggeringly, to defend himself. Then with a gasp of astonishment, he saw that he was alone on the bank. The river, swirling past, gray in the dawn light, gave no sign. Only, many yards down out from shore, there came a single convulsive splash, such as might have been made by a jumping fish. So Earless Jake Rogers went to his last accounting.

Tom's thoughts flashed back to Cub. He found the moccasin, refilled it with water and was hurrying up the bank when he heard voices in the woods to the east. Like a rabbit he dove for cover in the gully mouth.

Four or five men were crashing through the brush from the direction of the clearing, evidently drawn by the sound of Rogers' shot. They passed, a dozen yards below, and went down the bank toward the water's edge. As Tom wriggled along the bottom of the ditch he could hear them behind him, running along the shore and shouting their leader's name. The dim light that was now sifting through the trees made the gully a poor hiding place, but Tom had no choice. He was thinking more of Cub's life than of his own safety.

He crossed the shallow stretch and after that was able to crawl more rapidly. At last he reached the place where Andy and the dog were concealed, and found that in his absence the riverboy had pulled several pieces of brush over their hiding place. Under this shelter he was lying, with Cub's head across his knees. The terrier opened his eyes at Tom's approach and tried feebly to wag his tail. When the water was put beneath his nose he lapped a little of it and seemed to feel better. Andy had torn a sleeve from his shirt, bandaging the dog's broken foreleg with a piece of stick. And in the meantime the blood had stopped flowing from the gash in Cub's head.

With the sunrise, horizontal beams of light began to filter through the trees. Birds were awake and singing on every side. It was Andy who noticed suddenly that there had come a lull in this flood of melody. As he motioned to Tom, the Pennsylvania boy gripped Cub's muzzle and turned his head, listening. At first all was silent. Then a twig snapped loudly, very close at hand, and a man spoke.

"Whatever 'come o' Jake, arter he fired that gun?" queried the voice.

"They was tracks in the wet sand," another man replied, "but I lost 'em, part way up the bank. Pedro's gone down a ways, lookin' fer the boat. Soon as he comes back an' we git a bite o' breakfast, I vote we go through here careful an' dig these young varmints out. I'll lay ten beaver pelts to a coyote's tail we'll find 'em layin' low here in this strip o' woods."

As they spoke, the two outlaws paused momentarily in front of Andy's heap of brush, then, to the boys intense relief, passed around it to the north and went on toward the clearing.

Hardly had their footsteps died away when Andy laid a hand on Tom's arm. "What is it—that noise?" he whispered. "Hear it? Like singin'—by gumption, it *is* singin'! Listen!"

And Tom, raising his head to the level of the ground, caught drifting snatches of musical sound, very far off and faint. It was not like the singing of one man, but like a deep chorus of scores of voices. Then a strengthening breeze brought the song to them in louder volume, and it was Tom's turn to grow excited. "That's French!" he breathed. "I got some of the words, then. Andy, it must be the fur fleet!"

Andy made no reply. He was pulling off his shirt, which had been white two days before. "Here!" he exclaimed, when his head emerged. "This'll show up against the trees. Take it an' go, quick!"

Three minutes later Tom had crawled out of the gully and was running up the shore toward a spit of sand that jutted out into the river. He dashed out upon it, heedless of the danger of discovery from the rear. There were boats coming down with the current—dozens of boats—some of them nearly abreast of him already, and he waved the tattered shirt to and fro above his head, frantically.

Did he imagine it, or were some of the craft heading toward shore? No, it was true! Two—three—four of the big pirogues had changed their course and were coming down, crabwise, toward his sandpit.

He ran to meet the first one as its helmsman brought it skillfully alongside the bar. A great bundle of skins filled the boat amidships. Four men jumped out from bow and stern, pulling her nose far enough up on the sand to hold her.

"*Comment, donc, mon fils?*" shouted one of the four, a huge, bearded trapper in a deerskin tunic.

Tom thanked his stars then, for the smattering of river French he had picked up in St. Louis. With the aid of occasional signs, he made the men understand, in a general way, what had befallen himself and Andy. The second boatload had now landed, and a third pirogue was swinging in above the bar. Kentuckians were these—sandy-haired and blue-eyed men, with long-barreled rifles. They beached their boat and ran to join the trappers following Tom along the sandpit. Their leader overtook the boy just as he turned down the shore.

"What's this, matey?" he asked. "Some of Jericho Wilson's gang follered ye up the Mizzoura, eh? An' Pedro—that dirty dog from down Natchez way? We know 'em. They's plenty o' rope waitin' fer necks like theirs down in ol' St. Lou'."

Tom motioned for silence as they drew near the steep part of the bank at the side of the clearing. He peered cautiously over the edge and saw the five remaining outlaws squatted around a smoking breakfast fire, thirty yards away. Climbing silently up, the whole line of trappers gained the top of the bank before they were seen.

"Put up yer hands!" ordered the leader of the Kentuckians

briskly. And the five miscreants, scrambling to their feet in confusion, looked into the mouths of half a dozen rifles and hastened to obey.

Tom did not wait to see the captives tied up. He ran through the woods to the gully and almost tumbled in on Andy in his exuberance. "Wow!" he gasped. "We've caught 'em, every last one—thanks to this!" As he spoke he pulled on over Andy's head the remnant of the once white shirt. "Tuck that signal flag into your belt, and let's start," he chuckled.

Cub had been asleep, and now, as Tom carried him tenderly back toward the clearing, he seemed to have regained some of his strength. The trappers had kicked out the outlaws' fire, bound them hand and foot, and were ready to start when the boys appeared. Two of the jovial fur men carried Andy between them on their locked hands. Within a few moments they had regained the boats, stowed their new passengers and shoved off. The fleet was still going past—big keelboats and swift pirogues and canoes—all racing downriver to get the high prices of the early market.

The little flotilla which had come to the rescue of the boys had made only a mile or two when Tom sighted the *Phoebe Ann* coming up stream, her square sail set and the familiar figures of his uncle and Brad Bunker walking up and down her poling planks.

The crew of the fur boat, in which Tom and Andy were located, backed water and came alongside, to the accompaniment of joyful shouts from both vessels. In almost less time than it takes to tell it, the boys, with their dog, had been transferred to the deck of the keelboat, and the Kentuckians had bidden them godspeed and gone on their way.

CHAPTER XXVII

THE LOCKWOODS did not travel far that day. By the time Tom and Andy had related a few of their experiences and eaten breakfast, the *Phoebe Ann* was abreast of the spot where she had been attacked the night before. There the boys were delighted to find their trusty dugout still lying on the bank, and it did not take them long to hitch her at the keelboat's stern once more.

An hour later the *Phoebe Ann* tied up at a convenient mooring place, and Tom and Andy turned in for a nap. The events of the night had wearied both of them so much that they slept late into the afternoon. The odor of sizzling buffalo steak waked them. Aunt Phoebe was busy at the fire with a big skillet of the savory meat, and a pan of johnnycake was browning over the coals.

It was a royal feast they ate that night. When it was over, and the moonlit evening had been passed by the reunited family in talking and planning for the future, all hands went to bed and slept soundly until after sunrise.

The next day passed without incident other than the usual trouble with sandbars. Tom, fully recovered from the strain of his experiences and with nothing worse than a pair of blistered heels to show for his "crowhopping," took a short turn at the poling now and then. Andy's ankle was still too stiff and swollen to permit his using it much, but otherwise he felt, so he announced, "as spry as a six-legged rabbit with a bullet arter him."

Carefully washed and bandaged, the wound on Cub's head showed signs of beginning to heal, and his foreleg bone had been set by the skillful fingers of Aunt Phoebe. "He's got a couple more good b'ar fights in him, yet," said Andy.

It was nearly noon on the third day after the boys' escape from the river pirates. Tom, coming to the bow end of the walking plank and preparing to sink his pole to the bottom, scanned the river ahead with keen eyes, and paused, looking intently at the south bank.

"Uncle Ezra!" he called, "have you got the spyglass handy?" There was a thrill of excitement in his voice, and he pointed eagerly at a spot two or three miles away, across the yellow water.

"See that little patch of color?" he asked. "What does it look like through the glass? Isn't that an American flag?"

"I believe it is," said Ezra Lockwood, handing his nephew the telescope. "We'd best head over that way and see whether it is a settlement."

Tom and Brad Bunker manned the poles with a will, and in another hour the *Phoebe Ann* was nearing a wide, pleasant cove on the south shore, where a log wharf rose out of the river, and a small flag fluttered cheerfully from the top of a rough pole.

Slowly the keelboat drew abreast of the wharf, and Tom, with an end of the mooring rope in his hand, prepared to leap ashore. Through the trees he could see four or five log houses in a clearing.

"Ahoy, there!" Ezra Lockwood shouted. And in answer to the hail, a big man in buckskins, followed by a fair-haired woman and two little boys, came out of the nearest cabin. Tom, already on the wharf and making the boat fast, suddenly realized that their faces were familiar. "Why, it's the Colemans!" he cried.

A moment later all the keelboat's passengers had landed and were exchanging greetings with their friends. Phoebe Lockwood and Mary Coleman clung to each other and wept a little with happiness, while the men locked hands, saying little but showing their pleasure in their shining faces.

Tom and Andy felt a bit awkward during these proceedings, and stood by waiting for something more in their line. It soon came. Mrs. Coleman hurried back to her cabin to set more places at the split-log table. From the fireplace in the summer kitchen was brought a great kettle of venison stew, and from the dutch oven a pile of steaming-hot cornbread.

Then indeed the boys came into their own. To say that they did justice to this frontier repast would fall short of the truth.

During the meal Charles Coleman told of their happy beginnings in the new country; of how they had been able to clear and plant only a scant acre the previous summer, yet had gathered such a harvest from the rich soil that they had an abundance of food to carry them through the winter; of the friendly attitude of the fur traders, and such native people as came near them; of the increasing number of settlers up and down the valley, and the generous neighborliness they showed.

The Colemans and the three other families in the same settlement had cleared some extra ground in expectation of Ezra Lockwood's arrival, and had put in the earlier crops for him. It now remained for the Lockwood party to choose a site for their house, and to build it.

The first matter was soon settled. With unanimous approval, Tom's uncle selected a little knoll, a hundred yards or so from the Coleman's cabin, and about the same distance from the river. That decision reached, Andy brought axes and a whetstone from the *Phoebe Ann,* and for a good half hour he and Tom worked over the cutting edges, till they were as keen as knives.

"Makes ye feel kind o' good, don't it," said Andy, "to start makin' a house to live in, right out o' the insides o' this bran' new country!"

"You bet it does," said Tom.

He rose, tested the edge of his ax with his forefinger, and walked to the nearest tree. Soberly he spit on his hands. "Here goes for our new home," he said. "Here's one for Pennsylvania"—as he struck his first downward blow deep into the wood—"and here's one for Missouri!" He completed the opening with an underhand stroke, lower down.

Andy, coming up on the other side of the tree, sank his own ax in the wood with a ringing sound. "How 'bout one fer ol' Kaintuck'?" he laughed.

"Right!" said Tom. "But here's one"—he swung hard and cut a great white wedge from the trunk—"here's one that covers them all—the United States of America!"

"Hooray!" yelled redhaired Andy. And Cub's deep bark seemed, too, to say "Hooray!"

www.ingramcontent.com/pod-product-compliance
Lightning Source LLC
Chambersburg PA
CBHW030635190726
48286CB00008B/2529